GW01339182

PRINCE ZAAKI AND THE ROYAL SWORD OF LUELLA

By Heba Hamzeh

Prince Zaaki and the Royal Sword of Luella is published under Imagine Books, sectionalized division under Di Angelo Publications INC.

IMAGINE BOOKS

an imprint of Di Angelo Publications. Prince Zaaki and the Royal Sword of Luella. Copyright Di Angelo Publications 2020. Textual copyright © Heba Hamzeh in digital and print international distribution.

Di Angelo Publications

4265 San Felipe #1100

Houston, Texas, 77027

www.diangelopublications.com

Library of congress cataloging-in-publications data

Prince Zaaki and the Royal Sword of Luella. Downloadable via Kindle, iBooks and NOOK.

Library of Congress Registration

Paperback

ISBN 978-1-942549-65-9

Hardback

ISBN-978-1-942549-75-8

Cover Design: Savina Daeanova

Illustrations: Tamar Volkodav

Internal Layout: Kim James

No part of this book may be copied or distributed without the publisher's written approval.

For bulk orders, educational orders, or wholesale discounts, please contact sales@diangelopublications.com

1. Children's Fiction

2. Juvenile ―― Fiction ――United States of America with int. Distribution.

Dedication:

To my three angels, Lulu, Ella and Zaaki.

Table of Contents

Chapter I	9
Chapter II	19
Chapter III	25
Chapter IV	33
Chapter V	43
Chapter VI	57
Chapter VII	61
Chapter VIII	75
Chapter IX	95
Chapter X	105
Chapter XI	113
Chapter XII	119
Chapter XIII	131
Chapter XIV	143
Chapter XV	151
Chapter XVI	163
Chapter XVII	173
Chapter XVIII	181

The Kingdom of Luella

The Royal Palace of Luella

Pink Crystal Rocks

Magnetia

Royal Stone of Luella

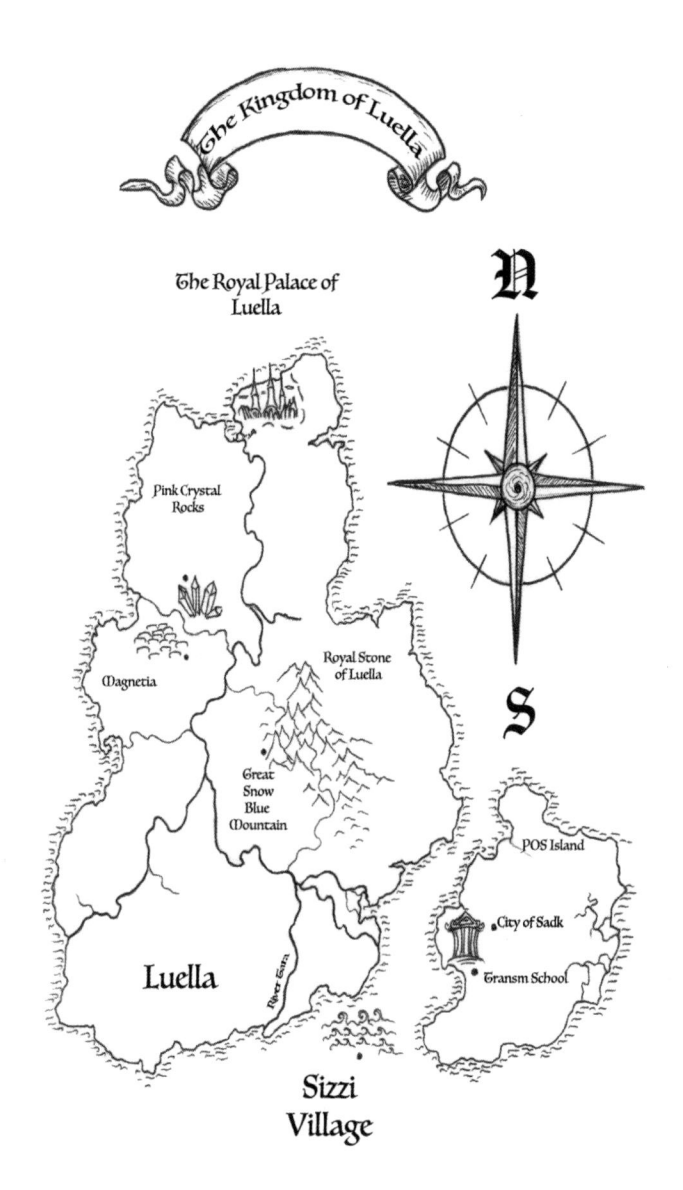

Great Snow Blue Mountain

Luella

River Esura

POS Island

City of Sadk

Transm School

Sizzi Village

Souls Sea

N

S

chapter One

I

Once upon a time in the magical Kingdom of Luella, there lived a young Prince, named after the great Saint Zaaki, who longed to travel and see the magnificent sights of Luella. As he was growing up, he yearned to leave the Palace and explore what lay outside the massive walls. The Royal Palace of Luella was built in the north of the Kingdom, because Saint Zaaki had wanted to reign at the head of his land. The four-storied building of fine black granite and olive-green marble domes was illuminated on special occasions with over a hundred thousand lights. The royal flag of Luella was white with an olive-green cross cut through it that signified Saint Zaaki the first, who battled the shadow dragon and saved the village in the mountains. Saint Zaaki was the great grandfather of Prince Zaaki.

Since Prince Zaaki was an only child, he was heir to the throne. His father, King Zok, decided that on the

Prince's twentieth birthday he would step down and Prince Zaaki would succeed him as King of Luella. He would rule over the wonderful province, full of vast, sandy red beaches, gigantic blue snow-covered mountains, and eerie, untouched caves.

The Prince had his wide balcony doors open to let in the radiant sun's rays, and a soft breeze ruffled the flowing curtains, casting a captivating golden-green rainbow across the Prince's suite. He loved the feel of the outside permeating his extravagantly large room. Prince Zaaki's suite had a familiar air of elegance and sophistication about it. While getting ready to attend breakfast with the King and Queen, the Prince was lost in thought over a matter he wanted to discuss urgently with his father.

"Prince Zaaki, I have finished your hair, will you be needing me this evening before your birthday ball?" asked his stylist, Broucher, as he added the final touches to Prince Zaaki's hair.

Prince Zaaki looked at his reflection in his long, golden, diamond-encrusted mirror. He was dressed in his favourite royal blue cloak, a black shirt, fitted trousers, and his fashionably pointy, knee-length boots lined with olive green diamonds in the shape of the royal crest . Luella's sword-shaped crest was that of a prince slaying a dragon, with a witch's face and two angels in the sky beyond the prince.

Prince Zaaki was fascinated by the history of his Kingdom; he had memorized all the stories of his grandfather and great grandfather; how they saved the people of the Kingdom from dragons, sorcery, and witches. King Zok would sit with Prince Zaaki at bedtime and tell him the tales of his forefathers as he was growing up.

As Prince Zaaki stared at his reflection, he imagined himself slaying a fire dragon and saving a village. Broucher saw that the Prince was preoccupied and coughed to interrupt his thoughts.

"Sorry, Broucher," Prince Zaaki said solemnly. "Yes, thank you. That will be all today. I will be fine this evening. You may go and see your love now, you lucky man. Bring your sweetheart and come this evening, it will be nice for some company while I dance with all the eligible ladies my mother has invited. I wish I could meet someone who will love and understand me. Not someone who is only interested in the title they will acquire if they become my wife. It's so hard to seek love and know that it is real!"

"Thank you, Your Royal Highness. You are a handsome young man and heir to the throne, so you could have any lady you want. You have servants who see to your every need. You are the lucky one. Your true love is out there. Just stop thinking about it and it will happen. May you have a great day today, see you at the ball this evening, and happy birthday, Prince." Broucher bowed to the Prince and walked backwards from the Prince's suite.

"Yes, yes," Prince Zaaki replied quietly, walking towards his balcony swathed in branches and flowers. He gazed onto the grounds of the Palace.

Prince Zaaki was not the lavish type; he dreamt of sleeping outside under the stars and listening to the singing red Catbirds. He remembered that the King and Queen had asked for his presence ten minutes earlier, so he hurried out of his suite to see them.

As it was Prince Zaaki's nineteenth birthday, he was having a special birthday breakfast with his parents on the floating balcony overlooking the glowing, purple-grassed grounds of the Palace, listening to the soft music made by the Catbirds. The sky was peaceful with the full sun in clear sight, and one dolphin-shaped cloud lingered in the west. Queen Tee-Tee loved to look after animals, so King Zok had declared the grounds of the Palace a home for all animals she cared for. Queen Tee-Tee's favourite was the silver-haired flying horse named Strongheart. Prince Zaaki looked down at the Zebflas, striped blue-and-gold flamingo-legged zebras, as they ran across the grounds, and the Girtigs, spotted giraffe-necked tigers, stretched for the golden berries hanging from the large pink trees.

"Father, I have been waiting eagerly to discuss something with you," Prince Zaaki said hastily. "As I am now nineteen years old, I will be King in exactly one year. I feel it is my duty to get to know my people and explore the Kingdom outside of the Palace walls. When I have seen our great nation, I will be more apt to reign."

Queen Tee-Tee smiled as Prince Zaaki explained his feelings, trying not to express her happiness until the King responded. As King Zok took a moment to deliberate what his son had said, he unbuttoned the first two butterfly-shaped buttons of his frilly white shirt.

King Zok stood and took his royal red cloak off, muttering, "Is it getting hot in here?"

"Well, the sun's rays are unusually strong this morning, dear," Queen Tee-Tee comforted her husband, rushing to take the cloak from his hands.

As they both sat down, she held his hand tightly and gave him a reassuring nod and a small smile. King Zok knew his wife gave her blessing, but he knew that the dangers outside the Palace were great. The Queen did not grasp the extent of threats and ill-wishes for the Tars.

"Father, you always say that experience is the best teacher. Let me experience what's outside these walls before I reign."

Finally, King Zok said, "My son, of course I want you to be the greatest King that the Kingdom of Luella has ever seen, and so I shall give you my blessing to travel across the land, explore the mountains and beaches, and meet our amazing people."

King Zok then looked at his personal assistant, Helpy, and summoned him over with his finger. "Prepare the royal luggage," he whispered. "I am going with my son. We leave tomorrow. Go!"

King Zok ordered Helpy away. Helpy jumped from the floating balcony onto a pink stepping stone, scurrying away to organise the packing.
Suddenly Prince Zaaki rose angrily.
"Father, I want to go alone. I don't need you to accompany me. Besides, who will run Luella? I cannot ask you

to leave all your duties and come with me. I will be fine. You have taught me well; I know how to handle myself."

Queen Tee-Tee interrupted, "You will take Strongheart with you. He is brave, fearless, and devoted to you."

"Thank you, mother. I will look after him well, I know he means a lot to you."

"Wait, wait," King Zok said quietly, still unconvinced that his son would be safe travelling alone. "If you want to go alone then I must sit with you and the Army General to plan your route. Go now to General Scarytis and start planning it, I will follow you shortly. You will leave tomorrow at dawn."

Prince Zaaki was thrilled. He took King Zok's hand and kissed it as he bowed. "Thank you, father, you will not regret this. Thank you, thank you."

"Yes, yes, now hurry along, no time to waste," King Zok replied, and so Prince Zaaki hurried to find General Scarytis, feeling content that his parents were allowing him to travel across the magical land of Luella.

Queen Tee-Tee walked over to her son. "Don't forget your ball this evening," she reminded him.

"I have invited all the royal families with eligible young daughters for you to meet."

Prince Zaaki disliked the balls his mother organised for him to try and meet his future wife. He imagined that most of the girls were pretentious and after only one thing, to be Queen of the Kingdom of Luella. Prince Zaaki adored his mother and her unconditional love, kindness, and understanding, hence he always tried to keep her happy by attending the gatherings. Queen Tee-Tee's elegance and beauty radiated throughout all of her royal events; she designed the ballroom, organised the themes, chose the decorations, entertainment, food, drinks, and always picked the guests to her liking.

"Zaaki really is unaware of what he is about to encounter, my darling wife," King Zok anxiously whispered. "I know he is brave, but I just hope that no evil finds him alone with no protection. I want him to go unrecognized and blend in with the crowd; I want no one to be aware he is of royal blood."

She looked up to comfort him, saying, "Don't forget we are Tars. Zaaki is a Tar, which means he is unbeatable, brave, and strong! Nothing can defeat us! Zaaki can defend himself and I know he will return to us safe and unharmed."

"General Scarytis, I have been looking for you all over the Palace. Please wait up," Prince Zaaki called out to the General, running down the stairs after him.

Scarytis turned around and saw the Prince approaching him, overly excited about something. He put his hand on his shoulder. "Calm down, Prince, what is it you want? I have to get to my men; we are sending some to the Great Snow Blue Mountain."

PRINCE ZAAKI AND THE ROYAL SWORD OF LUELLA

"Let me   catch my breath." Prince Zaaki paused to pant, and continued, "I am going on an expedition of Luella and I need your help to plan my route. I leave tomorrow, so we need to work on it now."

"Okay, I need half an hour. Meet me in my office then." Scarytis pressed a button on his watch. A black, circular board with a gold lightning bolt on the top appeared, hovering in the air. The General jumped on and ordered it to take him to the army headquarters on the Palace grounds.

Queen Tee-Tee walked into her bedroom and saw Helpy ordering his five assistants to pack the royal luggage. She sat on the pink-buttoned leather window seat and told Helpy, "You can stop that. The King will not be going anywhere, so please put everything back and go check on the ballroom. This will not just be a birthday ball, but the last ball before Prince Zaaki leaves the Palace on his quest. I want everything to be perfect."

"Hurry, hurry! Put evertyhing back, I want it done yesterday! Helpy ordered his helpers, clapping his hands twice to render his instruction more authoritave.

Helpy and his helpers finished and quietly bowed down to the Queen as they departed from her quarters. As the Queen shed her cloak and pointy purple shoes, she sighed softly, wondering if her son would be able to fend for himself.

Prince Zaaki and King Zok left the General's office and happily jumped onto the royal golden hoverboard that took them back to the Palace.

En route, King Zok instructed, "Zaaki, now that your route is planned out, you must get Strongheart ready. Come see me afterwards in the swords room."

King Zok dropped his son off at the stables and continued to the Palace. Prince Zaaki told the stable boys to get Strongheart ready for a long journey.
Prince Zaaki fed Strongheart a carrot and stroked his hair, softly but excitedly whispering in his ear, "Strongheart, we will be travelling up the Great Snow Blue Mountain, across the fields of Luella and along the surreal beaches. You will be my companion and together we will have a wonderful adventure. It's you and me now. Get a good night's sleep and we will leave at dawn."

Excited, Prince Zaaki made his way back to the Palace to find his father waiting for him in the swords room.

"Just on time, Zaaki." King Zok looked at Prince Zaaki as he walked towards him, and put his hands out, offering a long, gleaming, sharply-pointed sword to his son. "I want to give you this. I believe you are ready."

Prince Zaaki understood the magnitude of what his father was bestowing upon him; the Royal Sword of Luella, a great historical weapon privy only to Kings or Queens. Prince Zaaki felt the weight of the immense privilege.

"I am speechless, father. I am honoured you think I am ready to take on the Royal Sword of Luella." Prince Zaaki knelt before his father and kissed his hand.

"I don't think, my son, I know. You have already shown that you have courage to travel alone around our great land. I must warn you that not everything is as it seems. The caves of Luella are inhabited by dragons that have been dormant for a while now, but any evil can disturb them. If you encounter a dragon, summon help from the sword, which will only answer to you. Rise, Prince Zaaki and take the sword on your journey to becoming King of Luella." King Zok choked slightly at the end of his speech, his eyes welling up. A tear rolled down his cheek as he handed Prince Zaaki the sword.

chapter Two
II

Prince Zaaki left the swords room and made his way to his suite. Preoccupied with thoughts of his expedition, he heard a sudden crash at his feet and realized he had walked into the Queen's lady-in-waiting. Dusty old books she was carrying spilled across the floor.

"I'm so sorry, Your Highness, I didn't see you," the lady-in-waiting said as she lifted up her long green dress to crouch down and pick up the books.

Prince Zaaki helped her, apologizing for his distraction. Then peered at the lady-in-waiting, saw her dusting off her dress and sorting out her dusty old books, and smiled.

"Are you my mother's new lady-in-waiting?"

"Yes, Your Highness, I started two days ago. The Queen

is waiting for me; I must hurry, for I have to take these books to her at once."
"Yes, of course."

As she hurried along the zebra-striped carpet of the west corridor, Prince Zaaki watched. Something came over him and he abruptly called out, "You didn't tell me your name."

She stopped running, looked at him, and spoke softly. "Star. My name is Star."

The Prince nodded in acknowledgement, noticing that she had the most beautiful, honey-brown eyes before he continued to his quarters and Star made her way to the Queen.

The Queen waited for Star to disappear around the corner. She came out of hiding and hastily whispered, "Son, come with me to see the wizard Futuris. I have asked him to give you anything he deems necessary on your journey. He will guide you on how to summon for help and how to protect yourself."

Prince Zaaki agreed and Queen Tee-Tee clutched her son's arm, leading him swiftly to the basement where the wizard, Futuris, resided with shelves full of bottles and unusual objects. Futuris had a gift of foreseeing the future, so he knew that the Queen and Prince were about to arrive. He ordered the doors to open in the old language of Luella, Libnene:

Futuris summoned:
"Halla fatah ya bweb"

A brash wind began to howl, forcefully opening the doors before calming. Queen Tee-Tee and Prince Zaaki walked into the wizard's dark, gloomy basement. Once the doors shut behind Prince Zaaki and his mother, the room transformed into a very warm room with red brick walls and logs ablaze in a fireplace. In the centre of the room was a gigantic crystal ball, and by its side a book stand with a very old, yellow-paged book of magic. Prince Zaaki walked towards the book and started to look through it, dusting off the heavy pages, amazed by the spells inside.

"Ah you found the book of magic and power from within," Futuris said from the darkest corner of the room.

Prince Zaaki turned to see Futuris, but could only make out his profile and a long, dark cloak, so he slowly stepped away from the book and looked at Queen Tee-Tee.

"Futuris, come out and show your face," Queen Tee-Tee ordered. "We haven't much time."

An old man with a long white beard, piercing blue eyes, and a strikingly pointy nose began to walk towards Prince Zaaki. "This holds all the spells you could ever imagine and many more you could not. The spells will only work if you summon them from within and you really believe and want it. It takes wizards many, many years of training to perform a spell successfully, without backlash of any kind. I have enchanted the Palace and the grounds with a spell that allows you to use your hoverboard and glide magically through the air, but if you take it outside the grounds of the Palace it will not work. I am working on that spell now. Anyway, Queen Tee-Tee tells me you are going on an expedition."

Futuris held his long navy blue cloak on either side and walked over to Queen Tee-Tee, bowing down, keeping his eyes on her as he rose and said, "I am permitted to give you one spell that you can use at any time, or an endless supply of spells but which can only be used during the hour before sunrise and during the hour before sunset. It is your choice, Your Highness, but I warn you, choose wisely as there are many uncertainties in the Kingdom of Luella. Evil can come in many different shapes and forms, unnoticeable to the eye."

"Well, what kind of spells do you think I will require?" Prince Zaaki asked, looking at Futuris and his mother dubiously. He was looking for adventure in his journey, but did not really believe that he would encounter evil or danger.

As he thought to himself, he comprehended that having Futuris help him would be a good plan, and so he said, "Futuris, prepare me for the most danger you could imagine."

Futuris leafed through the book for the spells before going to his oversized crystal ball and chanting in Libnene, "Show me the Prince's first encounter with danger!"

Futuris ordered his crystal ball:
"farjene prince"s awwal muwajaha lil makhaatir"

As the crystal ball began to fog over and pictures appeared and disappeared, Futuris lifted his cloak up in front of the Queen and Prince and shoved them towards the door, saying, "Now I know what the Prince needs; I will have a book of spells ready for you in a few hours, so please come back then and I will show you how to use it. But now I need to be alone, for what I see, you will never be allowed to see."

Suddenly Prince Zaaki and Queen Tee-Tee found themselves on the other side of the wizard's doors.

"Now take me to my quarters, Zaaki, for I must get ready for this evening. I hope it all runs smoothly, and please this time be on time as it will be the last event I will hold until you return. I am going to miss you so terribly, but I understand you must do this. I hope you find what you are looking for and return safely to me." Queen Tee-Tee began to shed a few tears and Prince Zaaki hugged her, reassuring her that he would return unharmed.

chapter Three
III

After the most exquisite sunset, the masked guests arrived on golden gondolas, pushed through the steaming water by men wearing long black cloaks and cowboy hats with curved golden sticks. The guests were hovered two at a time into the glass-ceilinged ballroom. The pentagon-shaped room had black walls, and the floor was covered in white fog. Silver beams in the corners were engraved with the royal crest, and on the walls hung the pictures of the past Kings and Queens of this kingdom. As the guests entered in their gowns and suits, they were stunned by the beauty of the grand ballroom. Servants dressed in black and white costumes and masks, offered purple drinks and hors d'oeuvres from hoverboards. The Royal Orchestra was playing the Waltz, to which the guests danced. Floating balconies hovered near the ceiling, decorated with leather couches and fluffy cushions. People were laughing, dancing, drinking, and being merry when three loud knocks halted the celebration.

"Presenting King Zok and Queen Tee-Tee," announced the large speakers situated in every corner of the ballroom.

King Zok entered with Queen Tee-Tee at his side, landing next to the throne. As he sat down, the guests hailed him with applause. Queen Tee-Tee glanced around, looking for Prince Zaaki, and then beckoned her lady-in-waiting and whispered, "Where is Zaaki? Has he not made his entrance yet?"

Star nodded. "I will go find him at once, your Majesty."

Prince Zaaki sat on his suede armchair at his unseemly, pentagonal desk, going through the route on his map, calculating distances and time, when there was a loud knock at his door.

"What do you want? I'm busy!"

"Your Royal Highness, the guests have arrived, and your mother and father are asking for your presence immediately," Star shouted through the closed door.
Startled that he had forgotten his own birthday ball, the Prince rose from his chair and walked to his closet, where he grabbed his long black cloak and sat on the couch to put his shiny dancing shoes on.

He glanced at himself in the mirror and said, "That will have to do."
He then opened his door, picked up his electric blue hoverboard, ran out, and saw Star standing there waiting for him.

"Hi," he muttered.

"Hi. The Queen sent me to get you." Star looked stunning in her long, backless silk ballgown. She was trying hard not to gape as she looked into his big blue eyes, hoping he would not notice that she was madly besotted with him.

"Well, jump on and hold on tight."

As Prince Zaaki whisked Star around faster and faster on his hoverboard, her ball gown draping just behind, she clutched the Prince tighter and tighter.

The Prince hesitated as he was about to reassure Star that nothing bad would happen, then stopped and decided not to as he enjoyed her arms wrapped around him.

Laughter filled the ballroom as the orchestra paused to prepare for the next arrangements. Prince Zaaki was being introduced to one Princess after the other, though unfortunately none were quite to his liking. As Queen Tee-Tee and King Zok introduced him to the King and Queen of Tranquily and their three hideous daughters, Prince Zaaki dreaded having to ask each one to dance with him. The King of Tranquily's eldest daughter, Teensy, was rather the opposite of her name, and her face would light up when she saw the hors d'oeuvres.

Prince Zaaki reluctantly put his left hand out and said, "Shall we?"

Teensy wiped her hands on the sides of her dress and nodded as she chewed her food. Prince Zaaki took Teensy's hand and began to dance with her to the slow fox, all the while captivated by Star's splendour. She stood by the Queen's chair, waiting for her next order, looking flawless with her golden brown hair tied loosely in a knot at the back of her head. After a few minutes, Teensy's sister, Glory, tapped Teensy on the shoulder and asked if she could dance with the Prince in an extremely eager, high-pitched tone. Prince Zaaki, relieved that he didn't have to dance with Teensy anymore, took Glory by the hand. He brought her round to face him and he gasped in shock when he saw her. Her eyes were too close together and she squinted so hard that the Prince couldn't even distinguish their colour. Her squashed nose had a huge red spot that looked as if it could explode at any moment. Her short, greasy black hair was littered with pink ribbons tied in bows. The Prince tried to see past her exaggerated style, praying she might have a humorous and attractive personality.

"Are you alright, your Highness?" Glory twittered in her bird-like voice.

"Eh yes, I was just astonished to see that you sisters are all as pretty as each other." He paused for a moment and continued, "So what do you like to do? Swim, ride horses, paint, hover-board?"

"Well I like to do my sisters hair. And I like trying on different dresses." Glory giggled.

"Ah. Have you studied the history of Tranquily, and how your Kingdom was saved from the Dragon of Darkness by your great grandfather? My history tutor gave me some books to read about it. I find it fascinating, and you?"

Glory stared at him blankly, not really understanding what he was talking about. They danced until the song ended, upon which Prince Zaaki bowed and took off before she had risen from her curtsy.

The third daughter of the King and Queen of Tranquily, Princess Rosy, was on the prowl for Prince Zaaki. She asked Star if she had seen him, and, though Star had seen the Prince retreat to an empty floating balcony, she shook her head.

"No, I haven't seen him. But if I do, I will be sure to tell him you are looking for him." Star hurried to one of the waiters and told him to bring her up to one of the floating balconies.

"Are you hiding, Your Highness?"

"No!" Prince Zaaki exclaimed quickly. Subsequently, he turned to look behind him, pleased to see Star instead of the Princesses, and heaved a huge sigh of relief.

"Do you have to stand by my mother's side all evening? Or are you allowed a dance?"

"Your Highness, I have to attend to your mother all evening. But she has gone to her stylist now for a touch up on her hair." Star looked at him, wishing and hoping he would swoop her up in his arms and dance with her.

The fifty-man orchestra began to play the salsa and, just as she had hoped, Prince Zaaki walked towards her. He softly lifted her left hand, placing it on his right shoulder, and began to dance with her. They gazed silently into each other's eyes, both wishing that the song would never end. Oblivious to the time that had passed, they danced to three different pieces before Star peeked over the side of the balcony and noticed the Queen was returning to her chair with King Zok.

Star stopped dancing and spoke hastily. "I must return to my duties. Please take me back down to the ball."

"The irony of my life is unbelievable," Prince Zaaki said, shaking his head. "I just can't believe that I find you, just as I am about to leave on a terribly long expedition. Promise me one thing?"

"Anything for you, Your Highness," Star accepted.

"Firstly, stop calling me your Highness, my name is Zaaki. Secondly, will you wait for me until I return from my journey?" He took her hands and raised them to his heart, impatiently awaiting her response.

"Your High   I mean Zaaki, I am not going anywhere unless it is ordered by the Queen." Star smiled and Prince Zaaki took her to the Queen, utterly elated and quietly in love.

As anticipated, the music stopped and the loudspeakers summoned all the guests to the dinner hall, where a feast had been prepared along with a comical show featuring three jesters and a magician.

"Mother, father, thank you for this wonderful evening. It was spectacular, but I must go now and rest, for I have a big day ahead of me tomorrow. Mother, thank you for giving me Strongheart; I will keep in touch via the VS." Prince Zaaki kissed the Queen's hands and then shook King Zok's hand firmly before it turned into an embrace.

Prince Zaaki went to the wizard's basement and, seeing the doors open, entered to see Futuris waiting for him.

"I have been waiting for you. Now, come over here so I can show you how to perform these spells." Futuris walked over to his window and sat down on a cherry red couch with golden arms. Placing his hands in front of his chest, a book magically appeared. "This is your book of spells. Take it and read the first spell."

Prince Zaaki took the book and was overwhelmed at the number of spells. He read the first spell, which was extremely specific, and questioned Futuris, "How do you know that I will need this spell?"
As Prince Zaaki continued to look through the book, he noticed something. "Why are they numbered?"

"All I can tell you is that you will need these spells in the order they are numbered. Your Highness, I need to be sure that you return safely because you are the only heir to the throne and we need you to keep our Kingdom safe. When I look into the future, I see you as King and there is peace in Luella. I must ensure this." Futuris spoke firmly. He stood up and took the book from Prince Zaaki, turning to the fifth spell and instructing him to read it.

Futuris worked with Prince Zaaki to prepare him for his travels, but his final words stuck in Prince Zaaki's mind: "Guard this book with your life, for if it falls into the wrong hands, disaster will fall upon the Kingdom of Luella."

Prince Zaaki thanked Futuris and reassured him that the book would be safe with him.

chapter Four
IV

The early morning sun was rising in the east as the Prince took one more look back at the Palace. He patted Strongheart on the side and whispered in his ear, "It looks like the weather is on our side today. Ready for our great adventure, Strongheart?"

Strongheart neighed loudly and started to gallop. As he gained speed, his wings stretched out and his body lifted off the ground. Strongheart flew Prince Zaaki high above the fields of dazzling yellow and purple flowers. Prince Zaaki looked down at Luella's beauty and took a deep breath, soaking in the exquisiteness. The red sun blazed in the clear blue sky. Noticing that it looked larger than usual, Prince Zaaki lifted his left wrist, flipped the lid off his watch, and asked, "What is the hour?" Suddenly the bulky watch, with the royal crest engraved in its golden straps, spoke, "My master, it is ten past the hour of two."

"How far do we have until we reach our first destination?" Prince Zaaki asked.

A map of Luella appeared on the video screen, showing the Prince the way. "Master, my calculation is that you have five hours until you reach the bottom of the Great Snow Blue Mountain."

"Thank you, VS, that will be all for now. Strongheart, we should arrive before sunset. Not long to go now. We shall rest by River Tara soon." Prince Zaaki noticed that Strongheart's strong purple colour was fading slightly, signaling that he needed rest and food.

Three long hours later, Prince Zaaki recognized the River Tara in the far distance, surrounded by huge, bright pink crystals and dozens of small thatched villas built on wooden logs. Prince Zaaki knew that if he followed the River Tara east, it would eventually lead him to the red sandy beaches of Luella, and if he continued west along the river he would quickly reach the Great Snow Blue Mountain. Prince Zaaki sat on Strongheart, stunned at the panoramic beauty of the river sparkling under the sun's blazing red rays. Strongheart neighed loudly when he saw the fast-flowing water and flew as fast as he could to reach it and quench his thirst.

"Slow down, we must make sure that it is safe. Land over there." Prince Zaaki pointed to a secluded spot behind a large crystal rock, and Strongheart obediently began his descent.
Strongheart landed Prince Zaaki behind a magnificent, sparkling pink crystal whose reflection glistened in the

river, making it appear as if its floor was completely masked in dazzling crystals. Prince Zaaki jumped off Strongheart's back and began to examine the scenery around him. When he was confident that no one was around, he unstrapped his golden flask from Strongheart's saddle and began to drink. As he drank, he noticed something from the corner of his eye. Erring on the side of caution, he subtly drew his sword and stood in position to attack. He could hear faint footsteps behind a rock. As Prince Zaaki walked towards the rock, three Magnetians jumped out and surrounded him.

One of the three men began to speak in a deep, croaky voice. "Well, well, well, what do we have here? A count? No a lord? No "

He paused to examine the outsider, looking for a crest. "Look, men. We are in the presence of a Prince."

While Prince Zaaki was being interrogated, one of the men moved the point of his sword up to his throat and held it there. Strongheart quickly flew over and stood in between the Prince and the man, selflessly defending Prince Zaaki.

"What do you want? You look hungry." Prince Zaaki didn't want to fight with the Magnetians, so he spoke in a calming tone, remembering that they were peace-loving people who grew the best roses and looked after the crystals of Luella Kingdom.

One of the men began to groan, rubbing his hands together and nodding his head frantically. "We are very hungry; the dragon comes and takes our crops every evening at sunset and we are too scared to go out. What do you have?"

Prince Zaaki replied, "I have food and I can help you with your problem, but first put down your swords. I have come in peace and I wish you no harm." He returned his sword to his belt and lifted his arms up to his chest to display his peacefulness. The Magnetians looked at each other before the leader gave the other two a nod. They, too, sheathed their swords.

"I am Zaeem the Great, leader of the Magnetians, protector of Luella's great crystals," Zaeem stated boldly, moving forward. He was a big man with a moustache and short black beard, and curly black hair slicked back. He wore a dark purple metal head shield that covered his forehead, eyes, and nose. He wore tight black trousers with long, embroidered black boots, a white shirt, and a long fuchsia cloak with dark purple thread.

"These are my men, Protectius and Guardius. And you are a Prince?" Zaeem queried.

Protectius and Guardius were both well-built and wore fuchsia shirts, tight black trousers, knee-high boots, black waist-cut cloaks, and head shields engraved with a pink crystal. Protectius was clearly adored by the Magnetian ladies with his wavy brown hair, big brown eyes, and unshaven face. Guardius was not as blessed in looks, with receding hair, chubby cheeks, small brown eyes, and a squashed nose. He also had a metal left hand.

"I am Prince Zaaki, and this is my horse Strongheart. We are on our way to the Great Snow Blue Mountain, but we can help you before we proceed. Tell me all about this dragon," Prince Zaaki said curiously.

As soon as Zaeem realised that the Prince was royalty, he bowed in respect and ushered his men to do the same. "You are Prince Zaaki Tar, heir to the throne of Luella."

"You really don't have to do that, please, rise. No bowing is necessary."

"You should not be here; it is nearly sunset and the dragon will be on his way. Follow us. Hurry!" Zaeem tentatively looked up at the sky to investigate it thoroughly.

"This way," Protectius said, knowing the exact routine of the dragon. "He always comes from over there. Tell your horse not to fly now, we don't want to attract attention to ourselves."

Protectius took the lead, followed by Zaeem, Prince Zaaki, Strongheart, and Guardius at the back. They scurried through the dense field of rocks as tall as chestnut trees, manoeuvring from left to right. A loud growl sounded and Zaeem pressed a finger to his mouth.

"We are nearly there, quick, quick!" he murmured urgently.

They approached a single, enormous pink crystal surrounded by pink roses. Zaeem placed his left hand into a dent on the side of the rock and a door slid open. They ran swiftly into the interior of a gigantic rock, which was unquestionably spectacular. After Guardius ran in at the rear of their party, the door shut behind them.

They proceeded down a seemingly-endless crystal spiral staircase.

"Good, now that we are safe, let us continue to my home," Zaeem said calmly, his voice echoing inside the empty crystal rock as he continued down the staircase.

They finally reached a glowing tunnel with pockets in the ceiling, from which the reflections of the crystals shone through. They walked a hundred yards before arriving at Zaeem's home; the pink front door, shaped like a bubble, opened automatically when Zaeem knocked.

"We all live in little caves under the crystals. The Magnetians used to live aboveground but, since the dragon's attack, we have had to build these homes to keep our children and families safe. My children have not been aboveground for a whole year now." Zaeem spoke angrily, sinking into his favourite amber armchair.

"I didn't know that Luella had dragons again. My father would not allow this. He does not know; I am sure of this," Prince Zaaki said in disbelief.

"How will the King find out when none of the army ever stop in our village to make sure we are safe? Since Scarytis became army general last year, we have never seen a solider here. Now if they come, they will find a deserted village." Zaeem's eyes filled with sadness and despair as he informed Prince Zaaki of what had happened to the Magnetians.

"Tell me about the dragon. I need to know everything you know about it so I can help you defeat him. Start at the beginning." Prince Zaaki pulled out a chair and sat by Zaeem's side.

As Zaeem began to tell the story of how the dragon came to Magnetia, his wife, Rosa, walked in and offered Strongheart some food and water. Stunned by his beauty, she stroked his long, silver hair as he sipped the water.

Zaeem's children, Bobby and Ginger, came running into the living room shouting, "Daddy, daddy, you are here, yippee!"

Bobby hugged his father around the legs and Ginger jumped into his arms with the biggest grin on her angelic face. Bobby started tugging on his father's trousers, took a piece of paper out of his pocket, and handed it to Zaeem. Zaeem unfolded the paper and gasped at the drawing, an unbelievably astounding resemblance to the so-called dragon that had terrorised them. Silently, Zaeem passed the paper to Prince Zaaki.

Zaeem lifted his son and quietly asked him, "Where did you see this?"

Bobby whispered in his father's ear; he had seen this beast a long time ago when they lived aboveground, wandering in the vegetable field. Zaeem planted a kiss on Bobby's cheek, praised him for the lovely picture, and told Rosa to take the children to their bedroom.

"This is not a dragon. I have never seen this creature in any of the books I have studied. It has the face of a human being and a silvery viperfish body. Its wings and teeth look deadly. Did your son capture the exact similarities of this creature?" Prince Zaaki looked at Zaeem and his men for a response.

They all nodded in agreement.

"How do we stop it?" Protectius asked of Prince Zaaki. "It flies down and destroys our fields, and soon it will destroy our crystals. Our energy supply comes from our crystals, and the Palace and all the other villages in the Kingdom use this energy supply!"

"This Viper Dragon must be stopped, I agree," Prince Zaaki said.

"Let us have dinner now, and then we will discuss our plan to slay the Viper Dragon," Zaeem suggested as he helped his wife set the table with potato-and-carrot soup and some crusty old bread. Zaeem gave his wife a kiss on her cheek and sat beside her while they all ate.

Strongheart nickered quietly to attract Prince Zaaki's attention. The Prince excused himself from the table and walked over to Strongheart, who stood in the kitchen drinking water from a large bowl.

"Sir, you are now the owner and protector of the Royal Sword of Luella," Strongheart proclaimed encouragingly. "You must help these people. You can fight this thing with your sword. You have been taught extremely well by your father. I will be right by your side and I can get you high up next to it."

Prince Zaaki beckoned Zaeem into the kitchen and explained to him how he would go up just before sunset tomorrow to defeat the Viper Dragon. They conjured a brilliant plan before Zaeem insisted that they spend the night in his home.

chapter Five
V

The following morning, Zaeem accompanied Prince Zaaki and Strongheart aboveground to show them the destruction that the Viper Dragon had caused, hoping to prepare them for their attack against the beast. The cauterized fields were dingy and black, with smoke still rising from the ground. The purple and pink trees stood naked, roasted alive, with ash covering the ground all around their charred trunks. A profuse smell of cremated grass and flowers filled the air. Prince Zaaki gawked in horror at this massacre as Strongheart flew them over the devastation.

"What does the Viper Dragon want? It cannot just be here to eat your crops. It must want the crystals wait a minute." The Prince thought for a moment. "You said that they source energy to the Palace and all over the Kingdom. Maybe the dragon wants to disconnect the whole Kingdom, which will make it easier to attack the

Palace without anyone noticing." Prince Zaaki stared down at Magnetia, worried that evil would invade his home and concerned that his parents were potentially in serious danger.

Zaeem looked intently at his village, completely obliterated by the vile monster. The only area that remained unharmed was where the crystals resided. "I agree with your analysis of why this is happening, and we must end it very soon, otherwise they will take the crystals, ridding us all of energy. Please help us destroy the Viper Dragon so that my people can return to carrying on with their lives, and I will personally be indebted to you for the rest of my life."

"The Viper Dragon must be working for a higher evil. Every book I ever read on the past dragons and evil beasts of our great Kingdom have always been the accomplices of a higher evil force. But who?" The Prince looked to Zaeem, his eyes filling with worry.

Zaeem used the sun's location in the sky to calculate the time, appreciating the urgency to retreat back to his temporary home.

"The sun will begin to set in one hour. Let us go now and get you ready," Zaeem said, and instructed Strongheart to take them to their underground refuge.

The Prince, alone with Strongheart in a large empty room in Zaeem's home, began to flip through the book of spells. The first spell was titled 'To Defeat a Viper

Dragon,' and next to it was a picture that remarkably resembled the picture Zaeem's little boy had drawn. Prince Zaaki concentrated on learning the spell, unaware that he was secretly being watched by Fred, hiding in a small wooden cupboard. Prince Zaaki pulled out his sword and stared at it, clearly remembering his father's instructions on summoning strength from the magical sword. Fred watched in awe as Prince Zaaki held his sword in his hands and recited the spell. The sword began to radiate a magical golden blaze that ran all the way up his arm, into his shoulder, down his chest, reaching all the way to his legs and feet. Prince Zaaki touched Strongheart and the glimmer penetrated Strongheart as well, covering him from head to hoof in golden luminosity.

"We are now ready! Let's go!" Prince Zaaki exclaimed as he jumped onto Strongheart's back and stooped slightly to fit through the door.

Zaeem and his men were waiting patiently in the kitchen. They followed Strongheart through the tunnel, up the spiral staircase, and emerged at the pink rock crystals aboveground.

"Zaeem, Protectius, and Guardius, this is where I go alone. You return to your families, close this door, and do not open it until I return."

Zaeem puffed out his chest, grasped Prince Zaaki's arm, and firmly shook it. "Good luck!" His eyes conveyed sincerity and hope.

"Master, come in at once, I hear the dragon approaching." Protectius beckoned Zaeem to step back inside. He grabbed Zaeem's arm, pushing him in towards Guardius, then took a small leap, landed by Prince Zaaki's side, and ordered Guardius to shut the door.

"I will help you defeat this beast. I want to help, tell me what you want me to do, Your Royal Highness!" Protectius proclaimed, bowing down to the royal before him.

Suddenly they heard a roar and Prince Zaaki positioned his finger across his mouth as he looked at Protectius. He searched the sky for the Viper Dragon and as he looked east into the sunset, he saw a swarm of black-clad bird men wearing shiny masks that covered their whole head, with two small rounded holes where their black eyes pierced through. They flew towards Prince Zaaki, Strongheart, and Protectius, carrying with them a silky, ultra-thin black sheet.

'Fly low and go over there, Strongheart,' Prince Zaaki directed telepathically.

Strongheart obeyed and navigated them towards an unusually large, glimmering pink crystal hidden amongst the rocks.

When the Tire saw Protectius, they flew directly over him and threw a black sheet, entangling him inside a cobweb like material. Struggling to get out, Protectius extracted a crescent-shaped dagger from his right boot. Before he could act, two of the bird men seized him up in the sheet and carried him away.

Prince Zaaki was monitoring the situation closely from under a crystal rock. He whispered to Strongheart that, on his signal, they were to fly below the bag carrying Protectius and seize him as he set himself free. Prince Zaaki watched the other bird men go towards the crop fields as the two hauling Protectius headed back the way they came.

"On three we go, Strongheart. We must bring back Protectius. Ready?"

Strongheart twisted his head to nod in agreement.

Prince Zaaki counted down under his breath, "Three, two, one," and Strongheart leapt out from under the rock. Strongheart lifted his wings and began to fly towards the captured Protectius. Prince Zaaki raised his sword to eye level, carefully grasping the lead on Strongheart's neck with his other hand, and began to recite an invisibility spell. He knew he had two minutes of the magic summoned from the Royal Sword, and therefore had to act extremely speedily in his rescue. The Prince narrated the spell in Libnene:

Prince Zaaki:
"Khalene ikhtefe ma kilshe bidaro"

The instant Prince Zaaki dictated this spell, a whirlwind of invisibility wrapped her long transparent arms around Prince Zaaki and his flying horse, twirling them in the air, around and around until they disappeared completely. Strongheart closed in on the Tire transporting Protectius.

Prince Zaaki whispered, "Protectius, cut yourself loose. I am invisible and on Strongheart. Strongheart will position himself directly underneath you in five seconds."

Protectius fell through the sheet, landing, invisible, behind Prince Zaaki on Strongheart. Strongheart flew towards the burnt crop fields.

"Look over there. The Viper Dragon with the rest of the Tire. Strongheart, get closer," Prince Zaaki ordered as he watched intently to see what the dragon was doing with the bird men.

The invisibility was about to wear off as they approached the crop fields. As they came up behind the Viper Dragon, Prince Zaaki noticed it was a female. He also saw a group of Tire digging in the ground, searching for something as the Viper Dragon shouted at them to work faster.

"Soon my master will have the ultimate magic, and no one will be able to stop him!" The Viper Dragon croaked in laughter, rubbing her hands together.
Prince Zaaki overheard the Viper Dragon but thought to himself, 'What is the ultimate magic? Surely it couldn't be the crystal rocks!' and began to recall a story his history tutor had told him when he was eight years old.

A well-dressed, skinny blonde boy sat on a window sill, looking out into the rain and listening to his history tutor recount a battle between his grandfather and an evil sorceress, Malicia.

"My dear boy," Histrek began lecturing. "Your grandfather, King Zudus the Great, defeated the evil sorceress and her flies. She wanted to rule your Kingdom by stealing our precious magical pearls that helped your great grandfather, Saint Zaaki, and your grandfather build this great kingdom. When King Zudus defeated her and her followers, he hid the pearls somewhere in the Kingdom of Luella. These pearls allow our land to flourish with fruits and herbs and vegetables. Most importantly, these pearls have enriched our land with energy. But, to this day, no one has ever found them. King Zok announced on your birth that the search for these magical pearls was to end. The people of Luella should be thankful that the magic provided them with food, energy, and pure water."

"Wow, Histrek. Did my grandfather really defeat her? How did he do it? Tell me all the details. Please, please!" Prince Zaaki begged, excitedly tugging on Histrek's long grey cloak.

"Your grandfather was very brave and went alone to defeat her. He had only his sword and Strongheart's father, Bravesoul. Bravesoul was the perfect companion for your grandfather due to his unconditional love for him; he protected and defended your grandfather until his end. King Zudus knew that when Malicia and her men, the Tire, stole the pearls from the Palace, they were headed to the top of Great Snow Blue Mountain. So Bravesoul flew him there and landed him by the famous Luelza Stone. Malicia, standing atop the great Stone, had begun her ceremony, transferring the magic from the pearls into her body.

"Just to explain these soldiers of Malicia's; they were

some kind of flying men with small, unusual, fly-like wings on their shoulders and piercing black eyes. They are referred to in my history book as fly men and were given the name, Tire, which in Libnene means the flying man.

"Anyway, back to the story. When Bravesoul landed your grandfather, the Tire flew at once to attack him. Bravesoul fought them all with his spectacular fighting skills and, one by one, knocked these fly men out. As soon as they hit the ground, they disintegrated into a pool of sticky dark red mucus. Malicia told your grandfather that he was too late and that the transfer had already started. Your grandfather reached for his sword, the Royal Sword of Luella, and summoned all the magic of the sword to come alive and help him defeat the evil sorceress.

As he lifted the sword into the sky, lightning struck, just missing Malicia. The most remarkable phenomenon occurred then as the clouds in the sky parted to make way for the Goddess of Life. The Goddess floated towards King Zudus on a white cloud, wearing a long, white toga draped in dazzling diamonds, and a golden crown engraved with ivory pearls, so brilliantly bright that you'd be blinded by the sheer luminosity. The Goddess of Life, Goddess Lulu, with the power of her mind, motioned the pearls into her hands, withdrawing the power that had entered Malicia back into the pearls. Malicia furiously began searching to see if any of the Tire had survived in combat, spinning in circles, faster and faster, until finally she let out a loud, ghastly scream.

She lifted off of the ground and raised her right hand

up towards Goddess Lulu, casting a beam of dark purple light that crawled through the air to reach the pearls tightly grasped in the Goddess' fingers . Goddess Lulu created a silvery wind that rendered Malicia's attempt unsuccessful, and Malicia fell to the ground, temporarily overpowered. King Zudus walked slowly towards Malicia and raised his sword up to her neck, asking her why she had become so evil. You see, Malicia used to be one of your grandfather's playmates when he was a little boy, about your age. She was secretly in love with your grandfather. He was very handsome and had many admirers but Malicia, when King Zudus married your grandmother, turned to evil and destruction."

Histrek went on to inform the Prince of how Goddess Lulu empowered King Zudus with an overwhelming skill of combat. Malicia, during a sword duel against the King, chanted a spell that summoned hundreds of her followers to her aid, but Prince Zaaki's grandfather could feel the power running through his blood and bones, and knew he could defeat them all. Malicia ordered her men to attack and she stepped back cautiously, watching King Zudus successfully ward off the Tire.

Bravesoul watched as his master flew through the air, kicking the fly men dead. Bravesoul noticed Malicia escaping and flew over his master and his attackers, blocking Malicia from fleeing. The brawl between Malicia and Bravesoul ended in the unfortunate death of the King's horse. King Zudus saw this grapple from the corner of his eye as he defended himself against the bird men and, smouldering in grief, finished off the last of the Tire. Enraged that Malicia had killed Bravesoul, he took one giant leap fought her victoriously. King Zudus fell to

Bravesoul's side and, as tears made their way down his distraught face, the Goddess of Life descended from the sky and put her hand on the King's shoulder to comfort him, handing to him the string of magic pearls.

Goddess Lulu told him to place the pearls where no man, woman, evil beast, or being could ever find them and reassured King Zudus that Bravesoul would be looked after and treated well. She then extracted Bravesoul's spirit from his body and placed her hand on his silky, silver hair as they both rose to the sky on her cloud and disappeared. The clouds shifted back into their original places and order returned to the Kingdom once again.

"Wow, I want to be like my grandfather when I grow up, and fight evil sorceresses and the Tire," Prince Zaaki said, proud of his heritage.

"Evil cannot stay dormant for too long, Zaaki," Histrek answered. "Your day will come."

Prince Zaaki was poised and ready to battle evil, knowing that the Goddesses of Luella were within his sword and that, together with Futuris' book of spells, he was undefeatable. The Prince knew that the bird men were the descendants of the fly men that long ago attacked his grandfather. Prince Zaaki jumped off Strongheart and ordered Strongheart and Protectius to back away and wait for his signal. Prince Zaaki stood right behind the Viper Dragon and tapped her on the tail.

"Well, well, well," the Viper Dragon sniggered. She

turned to face the Prince. "If it isn't Your Highness, Prince Zaaki."

Five of the Viper Dragon's bird men flew to her side and stood in combat position, each one brandishing swords in their left hands and shiny black battle rifles in their right hands. They circled Prince Zaaki and waited for orders from their leader.

"What are you looking for?" Prince Zaaki questioned the Viper Dragon as he cautiously pivoted to ascertain each of the Tire's locations.

Suddenly a group of Tire shoved Strongheart and Protectius in their backs, pushing them with their rifles towards the Viper Dragon. The Viper Dragon launched fiendishly, causing her to summersault through the air.

"My master will soon be the King of Luella, and he promised me that I will be his Queen. So, I order you all to bow down to me, NOW!" As the wretched Viper Dragon belched her words out, her bird men forced their prisoners to the ground with their rifles. Prince Zaaki bent his head down, maintaining eye contact with the Viper Dragon, before suddenly raising himself up quickly and kicking the bird man holding him down in his face. The bird man twirled in mid-air, fell to the ground, and disintegrated instantaneously. Prince Zaaki moved on to the next bird man who came to attack him, jumping in the air and kicking his attackers effortlessly until they all vapourised. The Tire that surrounded Strongheart and Protectius watched as their group was killed by one man, and thus flew away in fear, leaving the Viper Dragon alone with Prince Zaaki and his two companions.

Dusting himself off, Prince Zaaki progressed towards the Viper Dragon and calmly spoke, "Now, I think you should bow down to me." He patiently waited for her to bow down. "What is it you want? I know you think there is something here."

Strongheart situated himself above the Viper Dragon and Protectius stood behind her, pushing his dagger into her back while Prince Zaaki interrogated her. Unfazed by the dagger, Strongheart, using his magical power, blew ice from his mouth and froze the Viper Dragon's body, leaving exposed only her monstrous face. Prince Zaaki pressed his sword into her chin, knowing that she would only be frozen for a short period of time.

"Why should I tell you? You are going to kill me anyway," the Viper Dragon responded, trying to hide her fear.

Prince Zaaki pressed his sword harder against the Viper Dragon's chin, hoping it would compel an answer.

"Okay, okay. I was sent by my Master to find something. I do not know what, but he said that I would know when I found it. My master told me to search every inch of enriched soil. That's it."

"Who is your Master?" Prince Zaaki grilled the Viper Dragon, noticing that the ice was melting.

"I will never tell you that," the Viper Dragon replied, breaking free from the ice and rotating her head upwards.

The Viper Dragon flew a few inches above the ground to make eye contact with Strongheart for a moment, leering at him. Prince Zaaki shouted caution to Strongheart just as the Viper Dragon opened her jaw as wide as it would go and, with her long, needle-like teeth, grabbed Strongheart around his waist, digging her teeth into his body.

Prince Zaaki ran directly beneath Strongheart and the Viper Dragon and recited a spell of leverage to raise him up. Protectius tried to leap onto the Viper Dragon but was unsuccessful, and instead resorted to throwing his dagger at the evil dragon.

The dagger pierced the dragon's tail and, not wasting any time, Protectius then pulled out a long, curved sword from his right boot and hurled it at the Viper Dragon, aiming for her heart. The sword bounced off the Viper Dragon's scales and landed near Protectius' feet.

During this time, Prince Zaaki recited his spell in Libnene: "Give me the ability to fly like the birds."

Prince Zaaki:
"Khalene tier mitl il usfore"

Without further ado, Prince Zaaki soared to the level of the Viper Dragon, repeatedly commanding her to release Strongheart, whose legs dangled from the Viper Dragon's jaw. Prince Zaaki furiously began to slit her throat repeatedly from left to right and right to left, enraged that she would not release his horse. During the Prince's attack, the Viper Dragon frantically tried to hit the Prince with her long tail. She slapped the Prince across his face with her right hand and the force caused him to summersault backwards before he flew back to her. As he flew, he noticed the sun had nearly set, which meant that he only had a few minutes left before the spell would wear off.

The Prince hastily reached the Viper Dragon's left breast and, without hesitation, stabbed her twice, forcing her to release Strongheart from her jaw. Strongheart, slightly overwrought, flew down onto land to recover whilst keeping his eyes locked on the dying Viper Dragon.

Prince Zaaki's eyes filled with anger. "And now, to finish you off, forever."

With a sway of his sword, Prince Zaaki sliced off her head. The Viper Dragon's body fell to the ground and her head, emitting a high-pitched scream, landed on top of it. Silence followed.

Protectius scanned Strongheart for injuries, grazing his hands over his long, lean body. Relieved that Strongheart had only mild abrasions, he remarked, "Strongheart is okay! Well done, Prince, you did it! You killed the Viper Dragon and rid us of the Tire!"
Prince Zaaki, out of breath, lowered himself and stared at what the sunset had left behind, thanking the powers of the universe and his two companions for helping him defeat the Tire and Viper Dragons.

chapter Six
VI

The kids were running and playing hide and seek in the crystal fields by the River Tara, ecstatic that they were finally back above ground, free from danger. Zaeem, his wife, and Guardius stood on the porch of Zaeem's damaged villa, expressing their gratitude with a true Magnetian party for Prince Zaaki and Strongheart. The whole village disregarded the fact that they had to rebuild their village, instead jubilantly celebrating in the path that lay between the village and River Tara. The Magnetians were elated that they could safely return to their homes because of their newfound hero, Prince Zaaki.

All the Magnetians raised their glasses towards the Prince as they shouted out gleefully, "Hail Prince Zaaki!"

Prince Zaaki blushed, nodding his head in acknowledgement of the Magnetians' appreciation.

"I couldn't have defeated the Viper Dragon without Strongheart and Protectius. So please, raise your glasses to my companion, Strongheart, and my new friend, Protectius." Prince Zaaki graciously lifted his glass.

The Prince shook Protectius' hand and patted Strongheart, peering into the bag hanging on his back to make sure his book and sword were safe.

"Prince Zaaki, can I talk to you in private please?" Zaeem asked and then, without waiting for a reply, continued, "Follow me."

Prince Zaaki and Zaeem went inside Zaeem's home and sat down in the cosy, small living room, Prince Zaaki on a blue and orange couch and Zaeem in his favourite burgundy armchair.

"How can we ever repay you for defeating the Viper Dragon and allowing us to return safely to our homes? The Magnetians are indebted to you and Strongheart and because of this I have decided that Protectius will accompany you on your journey," Zaeem boldly stated.

"I am extremely honoured by your gesture, but I cannot accept. Strongheart and I will be fine on our travels. You need Protectius here, as he is a great warrior. I will feel better leaving this village knowing that you, Guardius, and Protectius are defending Magnetia."

"Don't make your decision yet, you leave tomorrow so think about it and let me and Protectius have your final answer in the morning. Now go back and enjoy yourself. Go!" Zaeem demanded as he remained sitting on his favourite armchair.

As Prince Zaaki left the room, he felt a rush of cold run through him. He turned to see if Zaeem had felt anything, and saw a small shadow disappear out of the living room window. Prince Zaaki hurried to the window, but saw nothing and dismissed it as a hallucination from lack of sleep.

All around, there was silence as the Magnetians slept in their homes for the first time in over a year. Prince Zaaki slept on the burnt swinging couch on Zaeem's porch, with Strongheart on the floor beside him. The night air was peaceful; there was an aroma of calmness restoring itself back into Magnetia.

Someone tip-toed onto Zaeem's front porch and carefully searched the bag tied to Strongheart's body. Strongheart flinched, startling the criminal, making him freeze with bated breath. As soon as Strongheart returned to his dreams, the criminal gently removed the book of spells from the bag and disappeared into the darkness.

chapter Seven
VII

Prince Zaaki, anxious to continue his travels, woke Strongheart up just before sunrise so that they could set off before any of the Magnetians awoke. He placed a note on Zaeem's front door to express his admiration towards the Magnetians, and then departed quietly.

Strongheart raised his wings and, with Prince Zaaki safely on his back, flew up and away.

Prince turned to his wrist and turned on VS. "VS, can you direct us to the Great Snow Blue Mountain, please?" "Master, I have been worried. Where have you been? Queen Tee-Tee has been contacting you and has recorded messages for you to see; would you like to see them now?" VS inquired.

"Yes, show me at once."

Queen Tee-Tee appeared on the screen. Her first message inquired about his health. The next three, Queen Tee-Tee greeted her son in a more anxious tone. The final two messages, she demanded Prince Zaaki to call and reassure her of his health.

"VS, please call my mother immediately," Prince Zaaki ordered, attempting to make himself more presentable by pushing his hair back off his unshaven, exhausted face.

"It is calling Your Highness, please wait for connection to be completed," VS explained to the Prince.

"In three, two, one   you are on VS with the Queen," VS announced.

Queen Tee-Tee, extremely thankful to see her son safe, began to ramble on about respect and how he must endeavour to check in every evening to help set her mind at rest.

"Good morning, mother, how are you and father? I apologize for not returning your call but I was in Magnetia 'til this morning, helping them fight the Tire and Viper Dragons. Does father know that the Magnetians have been living underground in fear for over a year?" Prince Zaaki asked angrily.

Queen Tee-Tee, horrified by the information her son had shared, asked Star, who was standing beside her, to call the King at once.

"Zaaki, my dear son, are you hurt or injured? I am

shocked to hear this. I cannot believe that General Scarytis was unaware of this situation with the Magnetians, how awful. Tell me, did you use any spells and did they work?" Queen Tee-Tee spoke softly, but sounded deeply disturbed.

As Strongheart approached an overwhelming gathering of mammoth blue mountains, he turned to Prince Zaaki and questioned, "Prince, what shall I do, travel up the first mountain or go further to the following mountain?"

"Mother, I have to put you on hold. VS, show me the route from our current position to the Great Snow Blue Mountain," Prince Zaaki ordered. "And do it quickly!"
On VS' screen appeared the route, and the Prince noticed that the valleys in between the mountains were full of unknown caves and swamps. Consequently, he instructed Strongheart to travel up the second mountain on his far left after referring closely to the map.

"Is my mother still on hold, VS?" The Prince asked.

"Yes sir," VS replied. "Shall I put her back on the video screen?"

"Promptly!" Prince Zaaki commanded.

The screen was very fuzzy and making a swishing noise. Prince Zaaki tapped his watch, but the screen remained unclear and full of silver dots.

"What's happening, VS? Please disconnect and try again," Prince Zaaki said.
"Sir, I am having no luck. It seems that the Palace's con-

nection is down."

Prince Zaaki looked up at the magical sight before him, at the phenomenal blue mountains living side by side harmoniously, gleaming under the sun's rays, and thought to himself, Why would the connection be down in the Palace? This has never ever happened before. The crystal rocks are safe from evil, supplying energy to the entire Kingdom. What could be affecting the connection?

"Try again!" Prince Zaaki exclaimed impatiently.

VS continued to work at getting a connection, but failed and suggested to the Prince, "They might be mending the connection at the Palace, so maybe we should wait a little before trying again, sir?"

"Yes, yes, you are right VS," Prince Zaaki responded quickly. "Let us be patient. In one hour, try my mother again."

Strongheart flew the Prince up the exquisite mountain full of trees in different shades of blue. At the bottom of the mountain, there were tall, light blue pine trees lined with talking Transparrots, as Girtigs pecked at the trunks.

"Look, Prince, down at that tree. The Transparrots are singing to the Girtigs," Strongheart said, trying to lighten the mood and calm the Prince.

"How unbelievably peaceful it is here. It is so beautiful and serene." The Prince began to take in the magnificent scenery, fathoming that all these years he had been waiting to explore his Kingdom. He sucked in a deep breath of mountain air and exhaled slowly, anxious to inhale more. In complete awe of his surroundings, the Prince noticed an oversized, emerald green rabbit, an Emerabbit, nibbling at the blue grass. He laughed as he remembered a funny story his mother used to tell him about the Emerabbits.

If you touched an emerabbit, luck would be on your side forever.

Queen Tee-Tee began her story as she tucked her son into bed. "I was playing by my house on a hillside near the Great Snow Blue Mountain when I saw something scurrying from one royal blue bush to the next. I was scared but wanted to see what it was, so I cautiously took little steps forward until a great big animal jumped from behind a bush and started chasing me. I ran in circles around the bushes, trying to hide from this creature, screaming out, 'Help me, help me!' Then, as I was hiding in a fluffy bush shaped like a great big pear, I peered through the branches and saw it was an Emerabbit. I remembered that the Emerabbits were lucky, harmless creatures, so I slowly came out of the bush and walked towards it, still apprehensive that it might jump on me again. As soon as I was a few steps away, it glanced in my direction and began to run circles around me, saying in a peculiarly annoying tone, 'You can't catch me, you can't catch me.' Finally, after stumbling a few times, I managed to swipe my hand across the Emerabbit's leg. Since then my family and I have been blessed with everything I ever wished for. I even thank the Emerabbit for giving me the luck of meeting my soulmate, your father."

The six-year-old Prince, still laughing at how his mother was scared of an Emerabbit, asked, "Mummy, are there still Emerabbits in the Kingdom of Luella? And if I touch one, will luck be with me forever?"

"Of course, my darling, but no one in six years has ever seen them," Queen Tee-Tee replied, placing a kiss on the young Prince's forehead and gently stroking his hair as he fell asleep. "When the Kingdom was attacked by dragons on your birth, the Emerabbits were frightened of the screeching noise that the dragons bellowed, and they have been in hiding since, not daring to show their faces on the mountains."

"Strongheart, you can now fly more swiftly as time is not on our side today," Prince Zaaki informed his horse. "The sun is going to set very soon and we need to find the Great Snow Blue Mountain."

"Very well, Prince. Hold on!" With these words, Strongheart picked up speed and rocketed through the sky. Prince Zaaki grasped tightly to Strongheart as he nearly fell backwards from the force of the speed.

Strongheart flew over the magical forests hidden in the blue mountains, where the most beautiful, exotic waterfalls gushed crystal clear water. Even from high above, the Prince could see the bottom of the transparent large river that lay around it. There were five equidistant waterfalls coming out of gigantic sapphire rocks, the powerful flow of water sounding of heavy rain, then flowing calmly into a serene lake nestled amongst tall tropical trees and overgrown plants.

Strongheart flew from mountain to mountain, slowing when they neared the colossal mountain. It was spectacular. Prince Zaaki's jaw dropped when he looked up at its' mammoth presence. Completely and utterly stunned by the vast beauty of this sparkling blue mountain, Strongheart lowered himself to the ground, allowing the awed Prince Zaaki to dismount.

"Prince Zaaki, I think I have a connection with the Palace," VS said, startling the Prince and Strongheart. "It is a weak connection, though."

Prince Zaaki lifted his wrist up to his face, hoping that he could see his mother.

"Hello, mother   father   I am standing in front of the amazingly captivating Great Snow Blue Mountain," Prince Zaaki said, eager to hear his mother's voice. "Mother, you never told me it was this beautiful. Mother   Father   can anyone see or hear me?"

There was no reply, just dead silence from the Prince's VS before it completely shut down.

"What is happening? Do you think something happened in the Palace?" Prince Zaaki queried, hoping Strongheart would reassure him. "We need to find out who is the master of the Viper Dragon."

Before Strongheart could reply, he was distracted by a swarm of oversized silver bees, Buzzers, hurtling directly towards them. The Buzzers commenced attack on the Prince and Strongheart, shooting hundreds of tiny honey rocks from their mouths.

Prince Zaaki, remembering that he had seen a spell to vanish these hostile bees, ran to Strongheart to retrieve the spell book from his bag.

"Where's my book? Oh no! Where's my book?" Prince Zaaki repeated, desperately searching for his book of spells.

Suddenly, a group of honey rocks hit Strongheart, causing Strongheart, with Prince Zaaki on his back, to fall and glued Strongheart's hooves to the ground. Prince Zaaki quickly grabbed his sword, fighting off the rocks still pouring down on them; he deflected the honey rocks back at the bees, fatally striking them to the ground. Strongheart raised his wings and used them to shield the Prince, also deflecting the rocks and knocking them dead. The last few remaining Buzzers, scared for their lives, fled rapidly.

The Sahaye Dragon, a slimy red snake dragon with a slithery tongue and the power of invisibility visualized and started to speak very slowly. "Hello Prince Zaaki, it is indeed an honour to be in the presence of royalty."

The Sahaye Dragon bowed down sarcastically to the Prince and then raised his head, still floating around

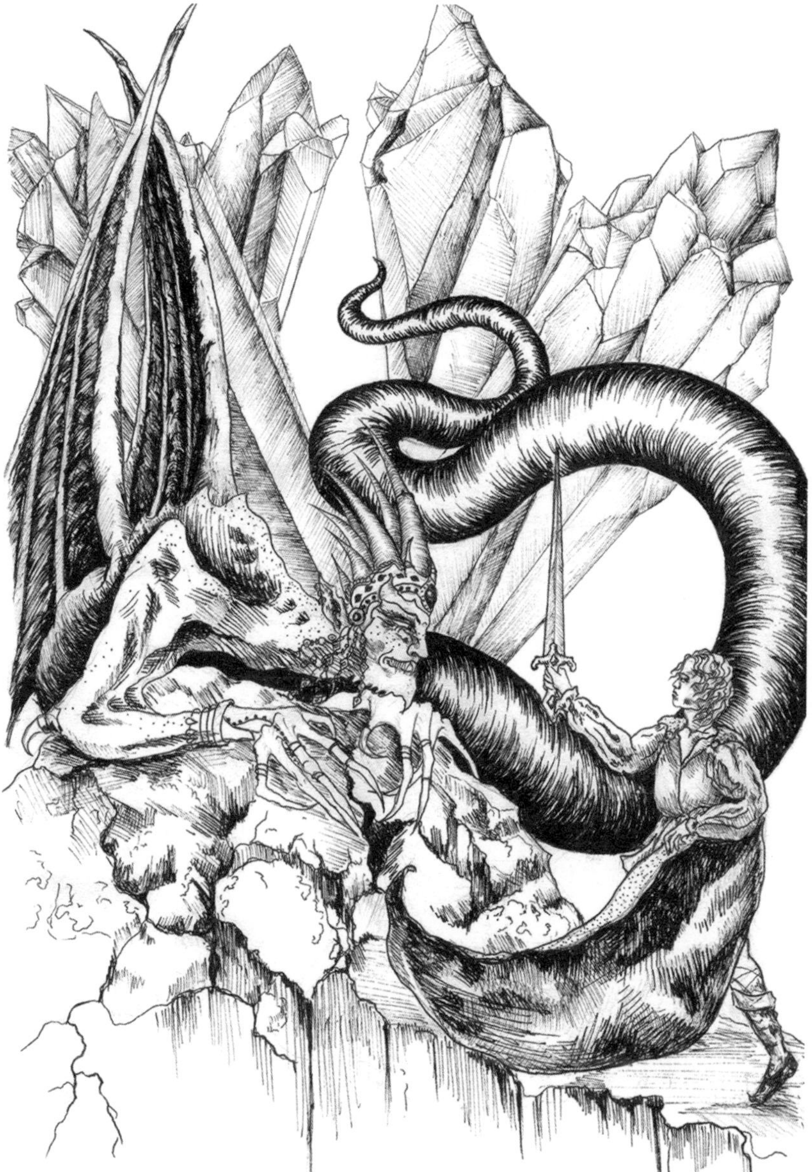

the Prince and Strongheart, lightly grazing the Prince's face with his tail as he passed. "You are in a bit of a sticky situation, are you not?" he taunted acrimoniously. "Do you want my help? Or are you too big to ask for it?" The Sahaye Dragon sniggered as he watched Prince Zaaki and Strongheart struggle to set Strongheart free from the sticky substance pinning him to the ground. The Sahaye Dragon's long lightning-shaped tongue shot out from his foul-smelling mouth and squirted red slime all over the Prince.

Prince Zaaki became extremely angry and slammed his sword down to the ground, forcing the tip of his sword to break the slime. A magical silver glow emanated from the Royal Sword and engulfed the Prince and Strongheart, releasing them from the slime and raising them to hover in mid-air. It twirled them around, removing all the slime, and then placed them a few metres away and disappeared with a bold, silver flash of lightning.

"Strongheart, are you alright?" Prince Zaaki asked as he quickly memorized his surroundings.

"I am fine, master. How are we going to defeat this dragon?" Strongheart asked, waiting for the Sahaye Dragon to reappear.

Prince Zaaki pondered for a minute on how he was going to defeat this strange, invisible dragon. After conjuring up a cunning plan, the Prince told Strongheart where to go and what to do. In the corner of his left eye, the Prince saw the Sahaye Dragon appear, flying at an extremely fast speed. The Prince headed towards him, raising his sword to summon the power to defeat the dragon. The Prince was furious that these dragons were trying to stop him from reaching his destination and began to comprehend that they must be acting on orders from a higher evil. He knew then that he couldn't kill the Sahaye Dragon, but needed to capture and interrogate him. After taking a deep breath, the Prince felt the power of the sword within him. He took a giant leap into the air and ran to the dragon as if he was climbing stairs, slashing the dragon's left wing with his sword. Dense red goo poured out of the dragon's wing as the Prince landed safely on the ground and ran to the back of the dragon. He jumped into the air once more and, with one swift move, cut the dragon's tail clean off. The tail fell to the ground with a loud thump, turned into black stone, and crumbled to dust. Prince Zaaki gave Strongheart a nod and Strongheart flew above the dragon, pushed him to the ground with his hooves, and pinned him down whilst the Prince walked around to face him. The Sahaye Dragon cried out from the pain.

When the Prince, holding onto his sword, began to wish for the Sahaye Dragon to truthfully answer all his questions, a bright light materialised in the sky and the Goddess of Honesty and Wisdom, Goddess Ella, emerged. She was dressed in a long ivory toga adorned with light blue pearls arranged in the shape of doves and wore a similarly-decorated golden crown. The pastel pearls matched the Goddess' eyes perfectly and her beauty and purity were apparent as she recited a spell that made the Sahaye Dragon tell the truth at once.

Goddess Ella:
"Ma fi kisebh min timak baah!"

As Goddess Ena recited her spell, she held her hands in front of her face, palms facing each other a few inches apart. A translucent white ball formed between her hands, spinning continuously. When the Goddess completed her spell, she threw the orb at the Sahaye Dragon. It disappeared upon impact, leaving a white glow encircling the dragon.

"My work here is done, Prince Zaaki. Your first three questions will be answered truthfully, following which the Sahaye Dragon will be relieved from my spell. Remember only your first three. Remember the stories your mother and father told you and act wisely, using your pure heart." When she was done speaking, Goddess Ella floated up into the sky, vanishing into the white clouds.

The Prince bowed his head, expressing his gratitude to Goddess Ella as she disappeared. He then anxiously turned to the wounded Sahaye Dragon pinned under Strongheart's hooves.

"How did you know where to find me?" he asked.

The Sahaye Dragon responded immediately. "I was ordered by my master to find you en route to the Great Snow Blue Mountain."

"What does your master want with me and the Kingdom of Luella?" the Prince queried impatiently.

"He is the rightful King of Luella and will be King very soon. As for you and your family, we are all on a mission to get rid of all the Tars."
"Who is this master you speak of?"

The Sahaye Dragon tried to resist the spell, but failed miserably and replied, "My master is the great General Scarytis, soon to be the most powerful man of the Kingdom of Luella, especially after I find the p   the p-p-p "

He stuttered, trying to stop himself from revealing what he was searching for.

Completely and utterly shocked, the Prince took a step back in fear for his parents and began to shake his head, finding it hard to swallow this information. "What are you searching for, is it the pearls? Is it?" Prince Zaaki demanded a truthful answer from the dragon.

The Sahaye Dragon sniggered.

"Your Royal Highness, what shall I do with the Snake Dragon?" Strongheart gallantly asked. "Let me finish him off!"

"Yes, off with his head!" the Prince ordered brashly, moving away from the dragon to allow Strongheart to deal with him.

Prince Zaaki turned his VS on. "VS, try my father now. There is no time to waste."

"Yes, Prince," VS said. "I am trying to get a connection now, give me a moment."

Strongheart struck the Sahaye Dragon across its face repeatedly with his front hoof. After just a few moments Strongheart gave one final strike and the dragon's head tumbled off, raining red slime. The Sahaye Dragon turned to black stone and crumbled to pieces that were blown away by the wind instantly, leaving behind just the memory of the Sahaye Dragon.

chapter Eight
VIII

"Prince, I can't get through to the Palace." VS said.

"Yes, it's General Scarytis. He is not what he seems," the Prince quietly acknowledged. "We must go back to the Palace without any more ado!"

"But, Your Royal Highness, you will be putting yourself in danger. It might be a trap. Please think this through," Strongheart warned.

"We need an army. How long will it take to reach the Great Snow Blue Mountain, if we fly without stopping?" the Prince asked VS, vigilantly watching the sky for any attack.

"Here is the map, Prince Zaaki. We have half a day left. If we leave now, we will arrive by nightfall," VS spoke as the screen changed to show the map.

PRINCE ZAAKI AND THE ROYAL SWORD OF LUELLA

"Strongheart, are you in good condition? Can you fly, without any rest?"

"Of course, Prince Zaaki! Jump on! No time to waste!" Strongheart bellowed.

The Prince mounted Strongheart, placed his sword back in its sheath on his belt and, with a long sigh, lowered his head as he thought of his parents.

On their travels towards the Great Snow Blue Mountain, Prince Zaaki and Strongheart flew over a majestic array of rock dunes and craters, hidden amongst the mountains.

Prince Zaaki glimpsed two beings among the dunes, moving hastily from one rock to another.

"Strongheart, can you get me closer to the dunes? I think I saw someone down there."

Suddenly he noticed a rather large figure chasing them. Strongheart landed as close to the rock dunes as possible without alerting the danger of their presence.

"Come back here, I am not finished with you or your horrid child!" a deep, croaky voice bellowed from the darkness. "I will find you and when I do "

Prince Zaaki and Strongheart hid behind a rock dune as the two people approached.

A woman and a little boy ran straight into Prince Zaaki as they were looking behind them, to make sure they were not followed. Startled, the woman grabbed her son and brought him close to her.

"Don't be scared, I want to help you. Who is that chasing you?" Prince Zaaki spoke in a soothing tone as he tried desperately to calm the woman and her little boy.

"He killed my husband and now he wants to kill me," The terrified woman replied, shaking nervously. "He wants to take my son. Please help us."

"Why does he want your son?"

The woman paused to deliberate whether he could be trusted.

"Please," Prince Zaaki said. "I want to help. I mean no harm."

The woman began to tell her story with a quiver in her voice. "My son has a special gift and foolishly my husband entrusted this secret with this knave. At the time we did not know he was not to be trusted. Then, just a month ago, he disappeared. There was a knock at the door this morning and when my husband answered it, he was standing in the doorway." She paused to let out a little cry, then finished without delay. "He stabbed my husband thrice in the heart, so I grabbed my son and ran out the back door. Please sir, take my son with you. I do not need safety but my son does, please, you seem pure of heart, I beg you."

"No, I will take both of you. Now, do as I say, and you will be safe. Ride my horse, Strongheart. He will take you out of harm's way at once."

Prince Zaaki carried the woman and her son onto Strongheart's back and told him to take them to safety.

He wordlessly reached for his sword as he heard stomping footsteps closing in on him.

"I know you are here. I can smell you. Just give me the boy and be gone with you," the man called out.

Prince Zaaki stepped forward, pointing his sword at the beast's heart. "Who are you looking for?"

"Who are you? Get out of my way, fool!"

"I will not allow you to touch the boy or his mother," Prince Zaaki declared, but the man just laughed out loud.

"You, you are telling me what I can and can not do? I will crush you with my bare hands."

Prince Zaaki, up for the challenge, placed his sword back in his belt and they wrestled. The beast threw the Prince over his shoulders and punched his stomach as the Prince landed on the floor. Prince Zaaki ignored the pain in his stomach, regained his breath, and unleashed himself onto the back of the beast, punching his head. Propelled by his anger and hatred of this murderer, he jumped off the beast's back and powerfully kicked him in the calf. The beast flew across the dunes and landed face down in the dirty sand.

Goddess Lulu and Goddess Ella appeared, drifting closer to the beast on a white cloud, looking more alluring than ever.

Goddess Ella motioned her hand in the air, as if clasping the back of the man's shirt and picked him up off the floor; controlling him with her powers, she swung him around in the air at supersonic speed.

"What are you doing to me? Get me down, you imbecile! Get me down. What is happening to me?" the monster cried.

The Goddesses glided closer to Prince Zaaki and thanked him for finding this beast, better known as Lutenavious.

"Lutenavious is a very dishonest man. He finds children who have a special gift and kills their families, taking them and locking them away for his personal use. We found his hiding place and rescued all ten children he had captured but we were never able to capture him. He is not worth killing but instead he will live a life of fear in the cave prison and think about all the despicable crimes he has committed. Prince Zaaki, come with us." Goddess Ella spoke softly, as always.
"I must find the woman and her son."

"They are safe. I told Strongheart to take them somewhere. We will meet them there soon. Take my hand, Zaaki." Goddess Lulu extended her hand.
As Prince Zaaki reached up to the Goddess, unable to reach her hand, he miraculously reappeared by her side on the cloud.

"That wasn't me," Goddess Lulu spoke. " That was you. Your powers are coming through now."

"What do you mean, I have powers?" Prince Zaaki looked at Goddess Lulu in bewilderment, but she did not elaborate further.

Goddess Ella continued to hold Lutenavious and summoned her cloud to fly towards the cave prison. Goddess Lulu and the Prince followed. They all vanished in a puff of white cloud and appeared by the cave prison.

A growling noise intensified from the darkness.

"Vamolf, I have a prisoner for you, please come and take him," Goddess Ella called into the eery cave.

A wolf-like man walked on all four legs towards the opening of the cave. As he stood upright, he rose to an impressive twelve feet, and when he opened his mouth to speak, four sharp canine teeth visualised.

"Goddess Ella, Goddess Lulu, always an honour to be in your presence. Did I smell correctly? You have Lutenavious I have reserved a special cell inside just for him," Vamolf declared excitedly, foaming at the mouth.

"Put me down. Put me down this instance!" Lutenaveious demanded, petrified.

"Your wish is my command," Goddess Ella conveyed happily.

Goddess Ella moved her hand towards the cave and then

released it open. As she did this, Lutenavious was thrown into the cave and landed in front of Vamolf. Trembling with fear at the strange creature standing before him, Lutenavious pleaded forgiveness but Vamolf, knowing his atrocious crimes, felt absolutely no mercy and pushed him into his new home, a small, smelly, and gloomy cell full of barbaric surprises.

"Thank you Vamolf. Lutenavious, Vamolf has an appetite for flesh and every prisoner who has ever attempted to escape well, you understand. My advice to you is, listen to Vamolf and stay in your cell." Goddess Ella bid farewell to Vamolf, her trusted friend.

The Goddesses and Prince Zaaki vanished one more time, reappearing in a beautiful hexagonal courtyard surrounded by a great, white stone wall.

"I never knew any of these places existed. Where are we now?" Prince Zaaki asked curiously.

"This is Pos Island. You are standing in the courtyard of the City of the Sun and Divine Knowledge. No one knows this Island exists and certainly no one knows of the City of the SADK. This is home to the Zenith Temple, the Temple of Lulu, and the Temple of Ella. The Zenith Temple is where the TransM School is located, that Goddess Ella and myself run." Goddess Lulu was interrupted by Strongheart landing nearby with the woman and her son.

"Thank you. Thank you. You saved my son. I am your faithful servant from now until my death." The woman dismounted Strongheart, held the Prince's hands close to her face, and kissed them.

"My dear lady, I was just in the right place at the right time. You do not owe me anything. Stand up and tell me your names?"

"I am Abe and this is my son Baal."

"I am Zaaki Tar, and this is my companion, Strongheart."

Suddenly Abe realised that she was standing before royalty, and bowed her head. "Your Highness, I thank you for your help."

"Abe will help me and Goddess Ella run the school and Baal, you will be a student here. We have been waiting for you." Goddess Lulu placed her hand on Baal's shoulder.

In awe of the Goddesses and her surroundings, Abe happily agreed and followed the Goddesses, along with Baal, to the Zenith temple.

Prince Zaaki, glad to be reunited with Strongheart, patted him on his side and accompanied them to the Zenith Temple. They walked straight across the Hexagonal Courtyard, past the Altar of Truth, and entered the Great Courtyard where three temples stood. To their left was a cube-shaped temple, the Temple of Ella, and to their right was another, the Temple of Lulu. Both these temples stood on ten-metre-high seraphic podiums encircled by columns. As they progressed through the Great Courtyard, they came upon a beautifully eye-catching edifice; a pale pink temple with eight golden pillars standing at the facade, glistening under the sun's rays. Over the pillars sat one letter made from red Aswan granite; the letter Z.

"Welcome to the Zenith Temple. Abe and Baal, this will be your home now. You are on the land of the Gods and Goddesses. You are safe here," Goddess Ella promised.

"Prince Zaaki, Abe, Baal, and Strongheart, you are about to enter our school. The lessons taking place will seem strange at first, but try to open your minds beyond reality. Look into your souls as well as at what appears before you. Those that do not use their tongues, instead use their eyes to learn, will absorb the wisdom and knowledge to truly understand the process of life," Goddess Lulu briefly explained. Upon gazing at confused faces, she added, " Let us proceed, without any further ado. You will soon understand my words."

In amazement of this building standing on a podium, twenty metres higher than the Great Courtyard, Prince Zaaki gaped at the perfect alignment of its structure. The Goddesses requested that their guests step onto their clouds, which carried them over the staircase that led to the front doors of the magical temple. The Zenith Temple was erected in between the Temple of Ella and the Temple of Lulu, to the north of the Great Courtyard. The City of the SADK was built at the highest point of the Island, so as soon as they reached the entrance, they were amongst the clouds. The temple was protected by pale pink columns encircling it, all exactly four metres apart. Baal was fascinated with the engravings in the stone columns and, for a split second, thought he saw a picture of him with a thunderbolt in his left hand and the sun in his right hand.

The magnificent double doors that stood fifteen metres tall opened as Goddess Ella summoned them with a nod. The Goddesses showed their guests the school, passing a room where students were taught to hone their gifts. The mentor in this room, Xvisio, flew over his students' heads, changing from a human into a sneagle, with his long, electric green hair and bright yellow eyes. Xvisio challenged his students to embrace their gifts and reach their potential. Goddess Ella subtly poked her head into the classroom.

"Xvisio, can we have a word please? Outside," Goddess Ella muttered, so as not to interrupt the class.

"Yes, of course. Class, work on the last spell. I will be but a moment."

"Xvisio, I would like to introduce Prince Zaaki, Strongheart, Abe, and Baal."

Xvisio greeted the guests, but when he noticed Baal, he hesitated, smiled, and welcomed him as if he knew Baal all his life.

"It is indeed an honour, we have been waiting for you " Xvisio paused. "Baal."

Prince Zaaki was beginning to realise that Baal was someone very valuable to the Goddesses, and that it was of extreme importance to keep him and his mother safe.

They advanced on the tour of this special school, meeting students in the hallways.

A little girl, Karena, bumped into Baal as she was rushing to her next class. "Oh, it's my fault, I am so sorry."

Baal picked up her books and smiled at her. Karena moved her short brown hair out of her face and looked at Baal.

"Thank you. I'm Karena."

"I am Baal. Nice to meet you," Baal replied.

"Are you one of us?"

"What do you mean?" Baal questioned.

"Now run along, Karena," Goddess Lulu cut in.

"Yes, Goddess Lulu." Karena speedily walked away, after sneaking a glance at Baal. "Bye Baal."

Baal's gaze followed Karena as she disappeared down the hall.

Finally, they reached a floating room, which appeared to have no entrance or exit.

Goddess Lulu asked her guests to all hold hands with her and Goddess Ella and close their eyes. In a flash of light, they were transported into a seemingly endless room. The ceiling and floor imitated clouds and sky; a lesson in progress could be heard but **not seen**.

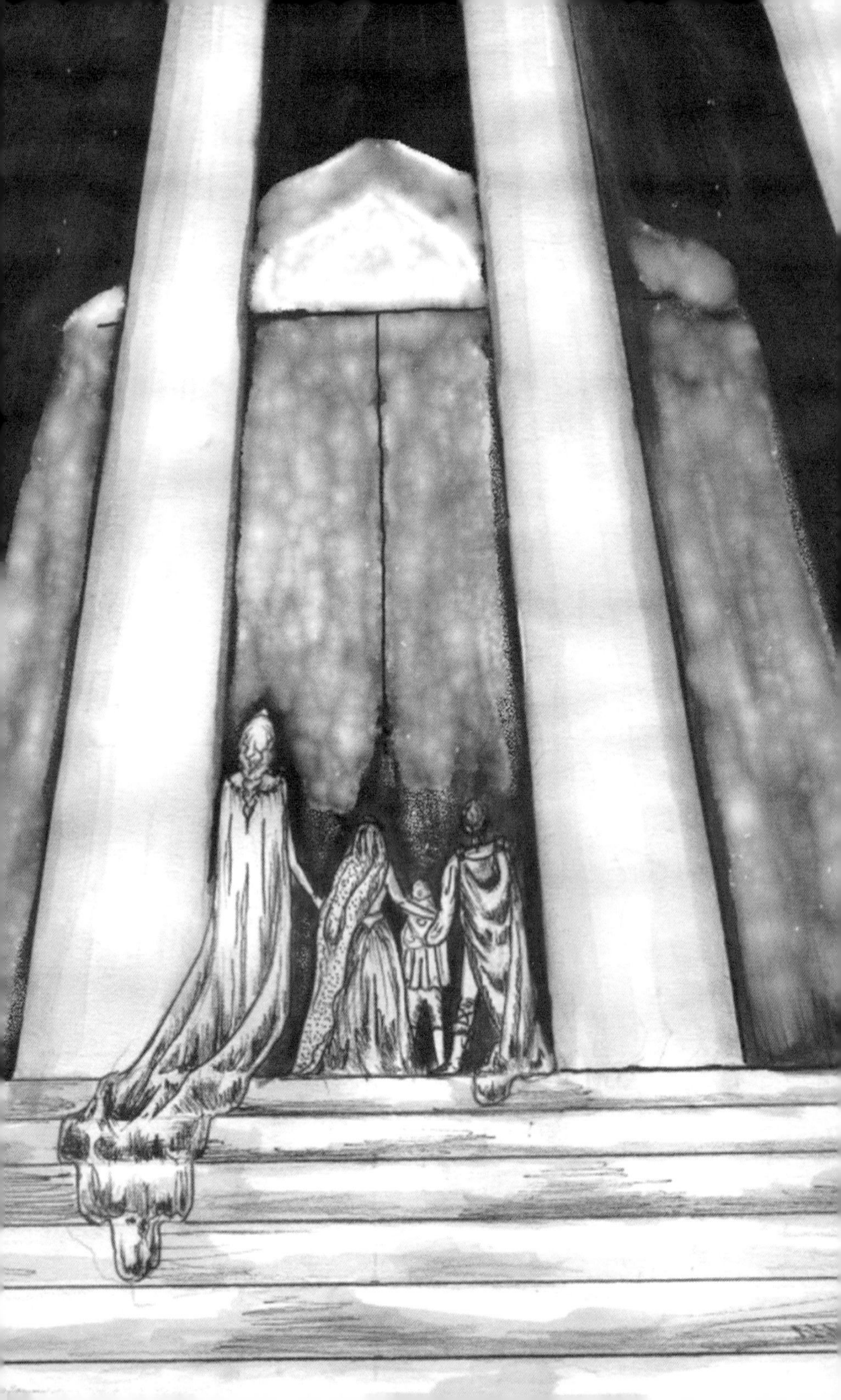

"Where are we?" Abe inquired, a little apprehensive.

"Don't worry, mother, I know this place. You are completely safe here," Baal comforted his mother.

"How do you know where we are, Baal?" Goddess Lulu asked.

"It's a feeling I have. It's the passage," Baal answered confidently.

"You are the one," Goddess Ella confirmed.

Goddess Ella and Goddess Lulu were filled with joy and emotion at the encounter of Baal and Prince Zaaki.

Prince Zaaki began to recollect a story he had read in the history of the Gods when he was younger that had mentioned a God, Baal. Prince Zaaki gazed at the little boy standing before him.

"I read about it, but I never thought I would ever see it. The passage of the souls. This island, it's Pos, the passage of the souls," Prince Zaaki marveled under his breath.

Goddess Lulu nodded at Prince Zaaki and told him that he was part of this school; the Z above the temple was missing the letters A, A, K, and I. A chill ran down Prince Zaaki's spine. He was overly eager to learn more and to help.

"Goddess Ella will take Abe and Baal to their quarters and help them settle in. Baal, you will begin class tomorrow and Abe, you too have a gift. Your gift is the gift of unconditional love. You find the goodness in everyone. You can see who is pure of heart and who is not. You are blessed with this and will teach it to our students. Prince Zaaki and Strongheart, please come with me," Goddess Lulu ordered.

Baal ran to Prince Zaaki, hugged him, and thanked him for saving his and his mother's life.

"I will never forget you," Baal said with a small grin as he walked away.

Abe graciously thanked Prince Zaaki and Strongheart with a look and a bow to the Prince before departing on her new journey.

Goddess Lulu touched Prince Zaaki's shoulder and Strongheart's nose. Suddenly they were standing in a twenty-five metre tall, thirty metre wide room. The walls were made of tantalizing gold stone, as was a ten-metre long marble desk encrusted with pink diamonds. The diamonds made the shape of an equilateral triangle. In each vertex was a letter: Z, L, and E.

Green diamonds at the centre of the triangle formed the shape of the Royal Sword of Luella. There was also a silvery picture of a God holding a thunderbolt in his left hand and the sun in his right hand. The sun, the thunderbolt, and a symbol on the God's belt resembling a wide U with a dot underneath it were made from yellow crystals.

"Come here, Strongheart, I have something for you,"

Goddess Lulu said kindly.

To the left of her dazzling desk was a huge plate of scrumptious food and drink for Strongheart, which he guzzled down impatiently.

"Prince Zaaki, now you are beginning to understand the complexity and importance of this place. It is the Gods' home first and foremost. Secondly, it is a school. The TransM School. We need your help in keeping this place hidden from the world, but at the same time, assist us in finding the gifted ones, the special children who should be encouraged to use the powers they have been given instead of hiding their talents within. You will come back and understand more but right now, the urgency lies in helping your parents, so I will send you back to your Kingdom and the place you had reached. You will not have lost any time," Goddess Lulu explained.

"I just have one question. When we were in the Hexagonal Courtyard, was that the Altar of Truth I saw?" Prince Zaaki asked.

"Yes but how did you see it? Ella?" Goddess Lulu asked bemused.

Goddess Ella gave Goddess Lulu a perturbed look before speaking, "Only Gods and Goddesses can see the Altar of Truth.," She paused for a moment. "Zaaki, you must go back now. We will discuss this later."
Prince Zaaki offered his gratitude to the Goddesses, before mounting Strongheart and disappearing within a golden cloud.

Queen Tee-Tee and King Zok were captured by General Scarytis and imprisoned in the basement with Futuris. General Scarytis commanded Futuris to stop all connections made with outside the Palace. General Scarytis chose not to imprison Star but kept her to serve him, giving her small errands to run, which included giving the King and Queen bread and water.

Star, carrying a tray with a jug of water and three cups, gave guards a stern look and told them to open the door to the basement at once. She hurried to where the King, Queen, and Futuris sat in a dark corner of the room and asked if they were hurt.

"We are fine. Go and take this to Zaaki, tell him the King and I are fine and well," Queen Tee-Tee whispered as she slipped a note into Star's right pocket.

"Star, go to the stables," King Zok instructed, cautiously looking over Star's shoulder to ensure that the guards were not listening. "Go to the one that is always left empty. Say these three words, 'Honeypower farjeh wijek,' and Honeypower will appear. She will fly you to Zaaki. Do not tell anyone, try not to look as if you are about to disobey the General, stay calm and focused. Now hurry!"

"I will not fail Your Royal Highness, I promise. Please do as the General asks and don't upset him, at least until Prince Zaaki rescues you," Star stated as she stood up and bowed to the King and Queen of Luella.

Star then looked at Futuris, gave him some water, and said softly, "Don't worry Futuris, Prince Zaaki will allow you to use your magic again."

"I have faith in the future King as you do; he is a Tar after all," Futuris spoke, coughing after each word, feeling drained.

Star departed from the basement and made her way to the stables, knowing that if she hesitated, one of General Scarytis' men would notice she was trying to escape.

"Star, Star where are you wandering off to! Come here!"

Star, upset and terrified, recognized that awful hoarse voice. She quickly thought of something and called out, "I am just going to get you some flowers to put in your new quarters. I thought they might brighten up your dull room."

"Well, let one of my men accompany you. I don't want you wandering outside the Palace on your own, it's not safe," General Scarytis said sarcastically, laughing out loud.

Star waited for one of the General's men to follow her, and then continued towards the Palace's garden. Star didn't know how she was going to evade this guard, but knew that she had to. Star, determined, lifted her dress and went down the steps that led to the side entrance of the garden. With the armed guard closely following her, she began to pick bright orange and silver roses. She gathered a bunch of roses carefully in her hands, and calmly informed the armed guard that she had finished.

As he turned back towards the entrance of the Palace, Star knocked him over the head with the garden scissors she had used to cut the delicate roses. The guard fell to the ground, unconscious, and Star headed straight for the stables as fast as her short legs could take her.

Finally, Star found the empty stable, stepped inside, and softly spoke, "Honeypower farjeh wijek."

Nothing happened, and Star wondered if she had recited the spell correctly. She began to twirl around the stable to see if Honeypower appeared. As Star began to recite the spell again, a small fog rose from the ground and filled the stable. When the fog faded, Honeypower appeared, a pink and silver flying horse with long silver hair and beautiful blue eyes.

Honeypower, gazing at Star, said, "I am only summoned if there is terrible danger. Who is in trouble?"

"The Palace has been taken over by General Scarytis. We must go and find Prince Zaaki, for he is the only one who can defeat the General, he is in position of the Royal Sword of Luella. You must take me now towards the Great Snow Blue Mountain. The General will soon find out I am gone, so we have to depart immediately," Star pointed out nervously.
"I am ready! Climb on my back," Honeypower ordered politely.

Without a moment to lose, Star did as she was told. Honeypower ran out of the stables, spread her wings, and soared high up into the sky.

Star looked behind her at the Royal Palace and saw the General's army frantically roaming the grounds in search of her. Relieved to be out of the Palace but worried about the King and Queen, Star calmed herself and concentrated on the map that Queen Tee-Tee had inserted in her pocket.

Chapter Nine
IX

Strongheart glanced at the Prince and asked him where he should land. The Prince looked down and tried to find a place outside the Snow Blue Village so as not to alarm the people sleeping peacefully. In the distance, at the top of the Great Snow Blue Mountain, the Prince saw something shining in the moonlight, but couldn't make it out. He ordered Strongheart to land near it, remembering a story his father told him about the tip of the mountain.

Strongheart flew silently over the village and arrived at the large, sparkling object. When finally he landed, Prince Zaaki jumped off his back and told him to rest, for tomorrow was going to be a long day.

The Prince walked right up to the object twinkling under the moon and grazed his hand across it, realising that this was the Royal Stone of Luelza. It was a rather obscure-looking black stone embedded with tiny clusters of glistening white diamonds. The Luelza Stone stood alone at the top of the Great Snow Blue Mountain, resembling a pyramid.

Prince Zaaki looked at Strongheart and found him fast asleep on the blue snow. He decided to rest on the side of the Luelza Stone until early morning and fell asleep the moment he lay down, dreaming of the evening his father told him the tale of the Luelza Stone.

"Are you ready for the story, Zaaki?" King Zok asked his twelve-year-old son as he walked into his room.
"Yes father, I am in bed and waiting for you. I can't wait to hear it!" a growing Prince said eagerly.

King Zok sat down by the Prince on his master bed and began to tell the tale of this magical stone.

"A long time ago in the mountains of Luella, there was a little boy, about your age now, playing near the top of the Great Snow Blue Mountain. He didn't have any brothers or sisters and so learnt to play on his own, conjuring up adventures and mysteries. One day, he decided to climb to the top of the Great Snow Blue Mountain and told his mother he was going to bring her back the cleanest, freshest blue snow. So off he went, and as he came close to the top of the mountain, he saw a black pyramid made of stone sparkling in the sunlight and something sticking out of the top; this obscure object gleamed so brightly and intensely, he couldn't see what it was. So this little boy continued to climb, until he arrived by the stone's side and climbed up the pyramid, covering his eyes with his hands from the intensity of the brightness. Reaching the top, he placed both hands on the long object that was stuck in the stone and, without thought, slowly pulled it out. He raised it in the air above his head with both hands and clearly saw it for what it was, a sword. This sword became known as the Royal Sword of Luella and this little boy was your great grandfather, King Saint Zaaki."

"Wow! That's my name. Carry on, carry on! Tell me more!" the intrigued Prince exclaimed.

"This bright light that encircled the sword began to encircle Zaaki and gave him an unbelievable power. He felt this power surge through his body, giving him strength and wisdom. After a few moments, two stunningly beautiful Goddesses appeared in the sky and told him that he was the protector of this land and that he was chosen to be the one who will help the Kingdom of Luella flourish and expand in population. Your great grandfather, King Saint Zaaki, knew now that this was his calling and he accepted this challenge. The Goddesses promised this little boy that, whenever he needed them, all he had to do was ask the sword for help and guidance. When the two Goddesses vanished, Zaaki climbed down the stone, which became known as the Luelza Stone, and made his way home. Zaaki was an incredibly determined young boy, and he later became the first King and Saint of Luella."

By the end of the story little Zaaki had fallen asleep, and so King Zok lifted the covers over the Prince, gave him a kiss on his forehead, and descended from the room on tiptoe.

It was early morning and Prince Zaaki was already awake, eager to go to the people of the Great Snow Blue Mountain to ask for help in freeing the King and Queen. He waited only a short while for Strongheart to wake and, wasting no time, they rode to the village. Prince Zaaki explained to Strongheart that they were going to build an army bigger than General Scarytis' army, hence they would be undefeatable.

"Firstly, we will get men from the Great Snow Blue Mountain," Prince Zaaki clarified to his companion. "And then we will follow the River Tara west towards the red sandy beaches and gather men from the Sizzi Village, and finally on our way to the Palace we will stop at Magnetia to gather Zaeem and his army of men. We have a lot to do in two days, Strongheart, are you with me?"

"Yes, Your Highness, I am with you all the way," Strongheart concurred.

Strongheart flew a little way down the Great Snow Blue Mountain to reach the village based slightly lower than the Luelza Stone. The blue snow that covered the top half of the mountain glistened spectacularly in the sunrise like shiny sapphire dust. The Snow Blue Village became visible under a lovely purple sky after the sun had risen. Prince Zaaki directed Strongheart to land near the centre of the village, so to alert the villagers as quickly as possible.

As soon as they safely arrived, Prince Zaaki disembarked the flying horse and walked towards the nearest home. He knocked on the front door.

A little voice responded from behind the wooden door, "Who is it?"

"I am the Prince of Luella and I am in need of some assistance. Could you please go fetch your mother or father at once?" Prince Zaaki commanded.

The door opened, but Prince Zaaki saw no one standing in the doorway. He called out, "Hello? Is anyone there?"

"Hello, yes I am here, how can I help you?"

Prince Zaaki followed the little voice and inclined his head to see a man, standing, under one meter tall, before him; a blue dwarf, wearing a purple suit with purple snow boots reaching his knees.

"Oh." The Prince paused, then continued. "I am here to seek your village leader. Could you please tell me where I might find him?"

"You are standing in his presence. I am the village leader. I am the head of the Snowites. My name is Blizzardis," Blizzardis said as he realised that before him stood the Prince of Luella, Prince Zaaki. He initiated a bow in respect for royalty. "Your Highness, how may I help you?"

"Can we come in?"

"Yes, of course. This way, please," Blizzardis said, directing the Prince and Strongheart into his blue living room.

"I don't have much time, Blizzardis. My father, King Zok, has been captured by General Scarytis and he is being held in the Royal Palace with my mother. I need to build an army to defeat the General and his men, can you help?" the Prince asked keenly.

"Your Highness, this is terrible news," Blizzardis, startled by the news, fell onto the navy wooden chair directly behind him, and hit his forehead with his right hand.

"How many men do you have in the village?" the Prince inquired.

Blizzardis thought for a few minutes before responding, "I have one thousand families residing all over the mountain, so I will be able to give you a thousand men, give or take some, and any sons who are old enough to fight. Let me make an announcement."

Blizzardis stood up and walked over to a device on his table, situated under a circular window on the wall that looked out onto the glistening blue snow. The device was a violet sphere with a small, bright red triangle on it; a loud speaker that Blizzardis used to communicate with his village. Blizzardis placed his squashed little nose on the bright red triangle and suddenly the sphere opened up, revealing an amethyst-coloured microphone, into which Blizzardis ordered all the men over the age of twenty to converge at the meeting point within the hour and the rest of the families to lock their doors and stay inside until they returned.

"Good, let us go now quickly and pick up the weapons that have accumulated here over the years. Your father ten years ago came to me and asked if I could protect and hide some things for him and told me that one day I will know when I will need them. That day has come!" Blizzardis lifted the carpet from beneath the Prince's feet, and then blocks of wood that were part of the floor. A secret passageway then appeared under the floor of his living room and he summoned the Prince and Strongheart to follow him.

Blizzardis led them through a pitch-black tunnel that connected his house to the inside of the mountain. Entering from complete darkness to sheer brightness within a few seconds, the Prince became overwhelmed at the exquisiteness of this spectacular place and stopped to stare, completely astounded at what lay before him.

"We are standing in the heart of the Great Snow Blue Mountain," Blizzardis informed him. "Your father and I built this connection alone and stored all the weird and unusual weapons that Futuris had acquired on his travels here inside the mountain. Your father knew not to trust anyone in the Palace; he didn't know who would betray him, but he knew that the day would come when evil would try to infect the Palace. What you see before you are the crystal rocks that make up the heart of this superior mountain. These are the stalactites and stalagmites of this immensity."

The rainbow of pastel colours that penetrated through the stalactites and stalagmites was breathtaking and the different shapes that the crystal rocks had formed was pure magic. Prince Zaaki was astonished by a pure white stalactite that resembled King Zok and another by its side that was the spitting image of Queen Tee-Tee. As his eyes proceeded along the stalactites, he noticed a cluster of rocks that resembled all the kings and queens of the Kingdom of Luella.

Strongheart gazed at a particular stalagmite that was gleaming from the water dripping from the stalactites. It reminded him of his late father, Bravesoul; it was even the same colours.

"Prince, Strongheart, please come and stand by my side," Blizzardis demanded.

As soon as Strongheart and Prince Zaaki stood beside Blizzardis on a monotonous green rock, Blizzardis tapped his foot on the ground twice and the rock they were standing on cracked off the edge of the floor and flew them down to the base of the mountain, between the stalagmites. Blizzardis jumped off the rock, walked to a pink, coral-shaped stalagmite, and lifted it up. A few inches from where the Prince and Strongheart stood, the floor opened to reveal a room full of weapons. Prince Zaaki, amazed that his father had been prepared for the worst, stepped into the room and gawked at the weapons displayed on shelves and cupboards. The Prince came to a very large object on the floor, completely covered by a black, velvet blanket.

"Quick, we must get these weapons above ground at once; my men will be waiting at the meeting point shortly. Strongheart, please come and stand by Prince Zaaki," Blizzardis ordered impatiently.

"How are we going to get all of these weapons out of here? Do you have some sort of spell?" the Prince asked sarcastically, letting out a brief laugh.

"Actually, you do! Remove your sword and place it in front of you," Blizzardis replied.

The Prince's laugh quickly ceased and, as he hesitated, Blizzardis said, "You do have the Royal Sword of Luella, don't you?"

"Yes, I am in possession of it," Prince Zaaki said, debating whether or not to trust Blizzardis. If my father trusted Blizzardis to keep this gigantic room of weapons safe, so must I. Thus he removed the sword from his belt and held it out as instructed.

"Prince Zaaki, repeat after me," Blizzardis said, and then recited a spell.

> Prince Zaaki exclaimed:
> "With the combined
> power of the sword
> and the power of the
> great snow blue mountain
> i summon this room move
> from inside to outside!"

With these words the room raised itself off the ground and then disappeared in a flash of silver lightning. Thunder crackled all across the village and the room reappeared outside, in the centre of the village, beside a long, electric blue pine tree with yellow pine cones facing upwards towards the red sun.

chapter Ten
X

After the Prince placed his sword back in his belt, he heard stomping and looked up to see a group of little blue dwarves marching towards him, wearing light blue snow suits over pastel blue long johns with black snow boots and hats. Blizzardis and his men blended in well with the snow-covered mountains of Luella. Blizzardis commanded his men to halt and began to introduce Prince Zaaki and Strongheart, explaining the King and Queen's capture and the Prince's plan to defeat the evil that had seized the Palace.

"So are you all with me?" the Prince asked the men standing before him.

They all hailed, "Long live the King and Queen of Luella."

"Everyone come forward and take some weapons!" Blizzardis yelled. He began to hand out sparkling silver and gold weapons; swords, daggers stamped with the Luella crest, bows and arrows, laser shot guns, and machine guns.

"What are these?" the Prince asked.

"Futuris brought these to me a year ago and told me to train my men to use them," Blizzardis explained. "They are called guns and they shoot out bullets at high speed which can seriously wound or even cause death."

Strongheart helped Blizzardis distribute the weapons as the Prince investigated a heavy machine gun. Unaware of its weight, the Prince took it off the shelf and nearly dropped the gun. Instantly drawn to its power and heaviness, the Prince strapped the machine gun across his left shoulder and continued to look at other weapons.

"Now that all the men have weapons, there is only one left. Prince Zaaki, this one is for you," Blizzardis walked to the object covered in a black velvet blanket.

The Prince waited anxiously to see what was under the cover as Blizzardis slowly exposed what lay beneath. A red metal object with wheels and wings came into the Prince's sight.

"This is called the Zoktransporter, named by your father. He came to me only a few months ago in this vehicle and asked me to guard it with my life as it was his personal favourite. Now I hand it to you, the son of the King. My boy " Blizzardis tried to place his hand on the Prince's shoulder but, failing to reach so high, placed his hand instead around the Prince's back and resumed, "Your father told me of your passion for the Kingdom of Luella and your good, pure heart. On his last visit he declared to me that you were ready to be King and fight for good. The King of Luella has faith in your complete judgment, hence we all are your soldiers and will follow your instructions and lead, Your Highness."

Blizzardis bowed down to the Prince of Luella and, as he came up, held out a fist, opening it to reveal a flashing green ring with one key hanging on it. The polished key was shaped like the Royal Sword of Luella and glowed like the blue snow sparkling under the bright sun.

"Strongheart, you will fly by my side, and Blizzardis, you will accompany me in the Zoktransporter," Prince Zaaki instructed, unlocking the door of the Zoktransporter. Prince Zaaki sat down in the driver's seat. Blizzardis sat in the passenger seat and began to explain how to fly the contraption.

The Zoktransporter's exterior was a metallic red, with the Royal Sword of Luella etched in silver on each side and two sliding doors that lifted above the ceiling of the transporter to reveal the interior. Inside, the Zoktransporter was outfitted with slick black seats, a triangular dashboard and gold and silver buttons and levers all over the dashboard and ceiling. The impressive vehicle was shaped like a triangle, with a pointed front and silver wings that lifted from the sides when the Zoktransporter was put into flight mode.

Blizzardis stood on his seat and stuck his head out of the window. "Snowites, follow the Prince and Strongheart," he shouted to his men. "Turn on your snow boots and let's go."

The Snowites all wore weapons strapped on their backs so they could hold long, silvery-blue metal sticks in front of them. When they pressed the button on the top of their sticks, their snow boots began to revolve under their feet, fitted conveyor belts on the soles carrying them swiftly across the snow.

"Now turn the engines on with this," Blizzardis said, pointing to a red lever.

The Prince followed Blizzardis' instructions carefully and began to drive the Zoktransporter while Strongheart flew at the Prince's side. As the Prince commenced take off, it started to snow, blocking the Prince's view until Blizzardis pushed a button that initiated the window wipers on the Zoktransporter.

The Snowites, undisturbed by the heavy fall of blue snow, continued to slide with increasing speed down the mountain, following the Prince, Blizzardis, and Strongheart flying a few meters above them. As Strongheart looked down at the Snowites he was astonished as they formed a diamond shape in the snow, moving swiftly but effortlessly down the Great Snow Blue Mountain.

After a few hours of flying, Prince Zaaki began to feel more comfortable behind the triangular red wheel. As he flew, he asked his VS to try and obtain a connection with his mother or father, but VS was unable to connect to the Palace at all,. VS returned his screen to the map, showing the Prince the quickest way to reach the red, sandy beaches of Luella. The map directed the Prince to descend from the mountains and follow the River Tara east towards the Souls Sea.

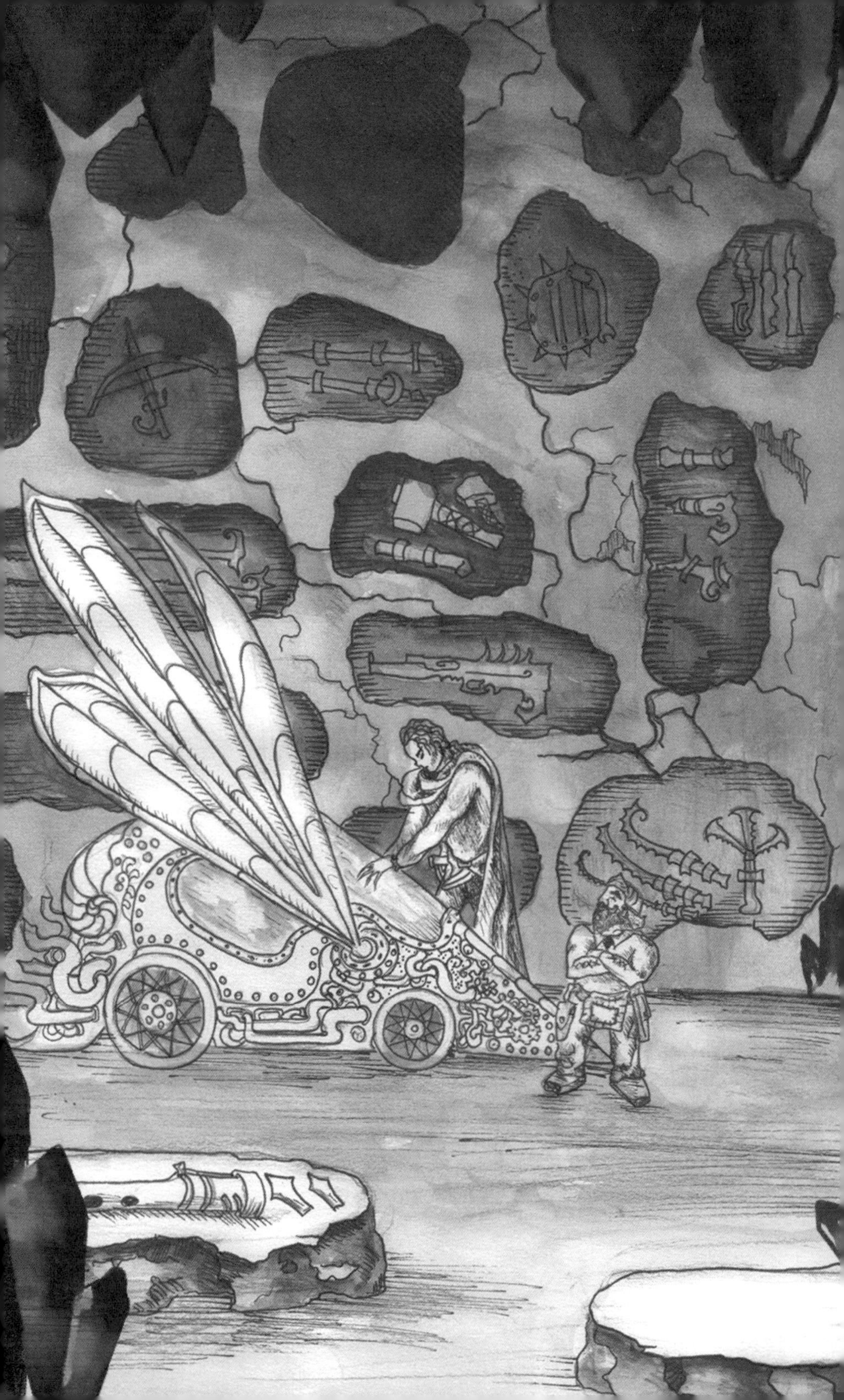

PRINCE ZAAKI AND THE ROYAL SWORD OF LUELLA

After the Prince and his followers reached the River Tara, the Prince switched off his VS, feeling confident that he knew how to reach his destination by following the river. Blizzardis informed the Prince that they should continue to fly through the sky, as the Snowites could keep up using their snow boots on the river. As the Prince turned left to follow the River Tara east towards the Red Sandy Beaches, the Snowites all stood by the edge of the river. They placed their feet together and positioned their snow stick in the middle of their boots, which transformed into water boots that could be manoeuvred left or right. One by one, the Snowites leapt into the river, pressed the button on the top of the blue stick they held, and suddenly were gliding on top of the water. The Prince noticed that the sun was about to set, so he turned on the lights of the Zoktransporter.
"Are you tired, Prince Zaaki?" Blizzardis enquired, reaching for the over-sized silver auto pilot button on the ceiling above the Prince's head.

"I'm exhausted but I need to keep going, my parents need me, and the Kingdom of Luella is in danger of being taken over by General Scarytis. We must press forward."

Blizzardis, wanting to help the Prince, advised him, "Let go of the wheel in three   two   one   now!"
The Prince let go of the steering triangle and Blizzardis instantly pressed the auto pilot button. The Prince found himself being driven by the Zoktransporter, and as he gazed out his triangular shaped tinted window, saw the Snowites smoothly gliding across the waters as if they were skiing on the slopes of the blue mountains. The

Prince turned to Blizzardis sitting on his right and gave him a nod of acknowledgement. Finally, the Prince glimpsed Strongheart, still full of life, flying through the sky.

"Sleep now, we will reach the beaches in the morning. I will wake you then, so rest your eyes!" Blizzardis reassured the Prince.

"Okay, I am just going to close my eyes for a little while. Wake me if anything hinders our travel," the Prince whispered as he drifted off to sleep.

Blizzardis, contented that Prince Zaaki accepted his advice, watched carefully out of the Zoktransporter windows for any disturbances that might halt them. It was a night of clear flying for the Snowites, so Blizzardis decided to rest his eyes for a short while.

Chapter Eleven
XI

"Wake up, Your Highness, wake up!" Strongheart bellowed, tapping the window of the Zok-transporter with his nose.

The Prince, startled, hastily opened his window. He looked worriedly at Strongheart. "What is it, Strongheart?"

With these words Strongheart kept quiet but flew upwards to reveal another flying horse flying by his side. It was Honeypower. Prince Zaaki, shocked to see Honeypower, noticed that she was carrying a peacefully sleeping passenger. Honeypower arched her back to try and jolt Star awake, but Star's whole body merely bounced. She was so exhausted; nothing could wake her.
"Are you who I think you are?" Prince Zaaki asked hesitantly.

"Yes, Your Highness, we finally meet. I am Honeypower, the Royal Flying Horse. I am accompanying the Queen's lady-in-waiting on her journey to find you and give you a message from your parents," Honeypower clarified.

"Blizzardis, can we stop for a moment? Tell your men to take a short rest when I land the Zoktransporter. Honeypower and Strongheart, please wait for me on the ground below," the Prince requested.
Blizzardis followed the Prince's orders and commanded the Snowites to take a break while the Prince went on to discuss his parents with Star.

Honeypower landed smoothly while Blizzardis guided Prince Zaaki in landing the Zoktransporter safely and smoothly. The Prince exited the vehicle, ran towards Honeypower, and stared at Star sleeping angelically on Honeypower's back, with her long golden-brown hair escaping her cloak's hood and covering one side of her stunning face. The Prince, contemplating how to wake Star from her deep sleep, swooped her up in his arms and carried her to the edge of the River Tara, laying her down amongst the purple grass. He took his cloak off and placed it gently under her head before caressing her face with the back of his left hand ever so lightly. In a soft voice the Prince repeated her name in attempt to wake her.

Meanwhile Strongheart, elated to see Honeypower after many years, began to rub the side of his head against hers. The affection they showed for each other was pure magic. Honeypower's eyes glistened as Strongheart whispered in her pink ears how much he had missed her.

"Star, are you alright? Star Star, please wake up." The Prince calmly caressed her face.

Star began to wake up, embarrassed to find that she was lying down with the Prince trying to wake her up. Impulsively Star sat up, knocking her head against the Prince's head.

"Oh, I am so sorry Your Highness, I must have fallen asleep while " Star stopped mid-sentence to search for Honeypower before continuing, "Where is Honeypower?"

"She's busy with her soul mate."

"What do you mean, who's her soul mate?" Star asked interestedly.

"The flying horse that brought you to me, and my flying horse, Strongheart, are in love and have been, long before you and I were born," the Prince comforted Star.

The Prince stood up and offered both his hands to Star to help her stand. Star thanked the Prince and, overwhelmed with relief, embraced the Prince. After a few moments, realising that she was locked in an embrace with the future King of Luella, let go and apologized for her behaviour.

The Prince, detecting Star was uncomfortable, asked, "Star, how are my parents? Where are they?"
"King Zok and Queen Tee-Tee have been captured by General Scarytis and are locked up in the basement with Futuris. Your father and mother sent me to find you and give you this," Star said, slipping her hand into her

cloak's pocket and procuring a letter, which she handed to the Prince. The Prince ripped the envelope open and read the letter without delay.

My Darling Son Zaaki,

Your father and I are well. The General has overtaken the Palace and imprisoned us in the basement with Futuris. The enchanted spell on the Palace has been removed, hence no VS signals can get through.

The King told me to remind you of your conversation in the swords room. Whatever happens to us, your fight is for the good of Luella. The sword is yours now, use it wisely. Go to the Snowites and ask for Blizzardis, he is a humble servant to the King. Visit the Sizzlites and seek out Goldy.

The General has thousands upon thousands of men with weapons and ammunition, so be careful.

Your father and I love you, my sweet, sweet boy.

Promise me that all you do is done with your good heart, and keep the Sword of Luella by your side.

This letter will be delivered by the only person your father and I trust, Star.

Your mother,
Queen Tee-Tee

The Prince read his mother's emotional letter and, tremendously determined to free his parents, called out to Blizzardis, "Gather your men, we are to leave now. We have a short journey until we reach Redsan, hurry!"
"Your Highness, I will tell the Snowites to be ready to depart immediately. If you would like Star to accompany you in the Zoktransporter, I can make my way on

the River Tara with the Snowites. I have taught you all I know of this contraption, now it is in your hands to drive this vehicle," Blizzardis said.
"Yes, alright, then you leave now and lead the Snowites straight along the River Tara and I will be with you shortly," replied Prince Zaaki, leading Star to the Zoktransporter by her hand. The Prince unlocked the Zoktransporter and Star, puzzled at this machine, stepped inside and sat in the passenger seat, gazing at the gold and silver interior.

"Strongheart, Honeypower, where are you? We are leaving now, this instance," the Prince beckoned.

The Prince jumped in the Zoktransporter and pressed a button to bring down the elevated doors.
"Hold on, Star. Ready for takeoff?" the Prince asked Star as he held onto the steering triangle and piloted the Zoktransporter of the ground.

"Take off, what do you mean take off? What, does this fly or something?" The confusion in Star's eyes escalated.

"Yes, something!" Prince Zaaki replied, anxious to show Star what the Zoktransporter could do.

Star's eyes enlarged in surprise at the capabilities of this weird, amazing vehicle. She gaped out of her window and saw Strongheart and Honeypower catching up with them.

"I can see Strongheart and Honeypower behind us," Star informed the Prince as he sped through the red sky.

chapter Twelve
XII

The luscious red sun shone its electrifying rays on the burning sand, as Starcrabs scurried to one side along the calm, transparent Souls Sea. The River Tara split into three rivers that all led into the Souls Sea, where fifty small villages hid, submerged deep in the waters; this is where the Sizzlites resided. The Sizzlites were Luella's sea protectors and their leader, Goldy, was a magnificently bold and courageous defender. Goldy was the guardian of the Souls Sea and head of the Sizzlite army. She was double the size of any other Sizzlite and had a silver glow that encircled the whole of her golden, half-human, half sea-horse body. She had pink eyes and long pink hair that covered the front of her body. The silver-coloured Sizzlites with golden locks of hair were also half-human, half sea-horse. They swam with their heads held high, their backs completely straight, and their sea-horse tails tagging behind. They built their homes in the breath-taking, colour-alternating coral at the bottom of the great sea. When the mood of the sea changed, so did the colour of the coral. The reflection of the Souls Sea was currently green, exuding serenity and great calmness. When the Souls Sea was sad, the Sizzlites were consequently sad as well. The Sizzlites were hypnotised by the mood of the sea just as the coral was.

Blizzardis signaled to the Prince and ordered his men to stop when they reached the point where the River Tara split into three rivers. Prince Zaaki flew the Zoktransporter down to where he could have a conversation with Blizzardis.

"Prince, which river shall we follow?" Blizzardis asked, determined to continue.

"Follow the river that curves to the right and then a few miles ahead you will reach the Souls Sea," Prince Zaaki explained to the leader of the Snowites, keen to multiply his army and free the Palace from the evil General.

"Stop your men on the beach and let them rest while I go and locate the leader of the Sizzlites," The Prince returned to a higher altitude and led his army to Redsan, the sandy beaches of Luella. Star looked at the Prince as he was driving this extravagant vehicle and thought to herself how good and strong he was. The Prince, manoeuvring the Zoktransporter, noticed she was staring at him.

"Are you alright Star?" the Prince asked.

Star quickly and ever so slightly tilted her head to make it look as if she was looking at Strongheart flying outside the window. "Yes, yes sorry, eh I am fine, Your Highness, just admiring your I mean Strongheart; he is a beautiful horse."

Then Star gazed at the Prince again and was lost for words. The Prince felt that she must feel the same way he does about her.

Strongheart tapped on the Prince's window and then gestured with his nose towards Redsan. At last, they had arrived. Blizzardis and his men glided across the water of the River Tara until they reached the Souls Sea, where they halted to rest on the red sand. The Snowites, unaccustomed to the heat, began to sweat and overheat until Blizzardis commanded them to remove their snow suits and boots.

The Starcrabs became terrified as they sensed danger and began to dig tunnels in the sand to hide from what was fast approaching. Strongheart and Honeypower noticed the Starcrabs scurrying into the sand and their instincts told them that evil was near. Prince Zaaki, blissfully unaware of the attack about to take place, landed the Zoktransporter and quickly exited to open the door for Star. As he helped her out of the Zoktransporter, he heard Blizzardis shout.

"We are under attack!" Blizzardis pointed to the monster in the sky roaring fire at them. "Quick, men, your weapons."

The Prince summoned Strongheart and Honeypower to him. As soon as Honeypower landed next to the Prince, he handed his machine gun to Star, giving her a quick lesson on how to aim and shoot. He then swiftly lifted Star onto Honeypower and ordered them to find shelter. Star, struggling to hold the weighty machine gun, placed it across her lap as she sat on Honeypower's back. Honeypower cast a look in Strongheart's direction, her big eyes voicelessly expressing her love for him. The Prince glanced around the beach and pointed to a huddle of sand hills in the distance.

"Honeypower, fly to the sand hills over there and guard Star with your life."

Honeypower nodded in agreement and, without further ado, flew Star to the sand hills, where they hid, peeking out from the sides to watch the battle.

"Strongheart, take me behind this creature!" the Prince quietly demanded as he jumped onto Strongheart's back.

Some of the Snowites were shooting at the yellow-spotted dragon with their machine guns, but she raced towards them uninhibited, spewing fire out of her mouth. The remainder of the Snowites began to fire arrows at the fierce dragon, but all rebounded off the dragon's skin and fell to the ground. Blizzardis was trying to aim his own bow and arrow at the dragon's heart when he suddenly saw Strongheart approaching the dragon from behind with the Prince on his back.

"Stop shooting at the dragon, you are wasting your ammunition. Find somewhere to hide. Go! Go! Go!" Blizzardis directed his men to the sand hills for safety.

The Snowites, some still in their snow suits and some in

their long johns, ran to the sand hills while Blizzardis tried to distract the dragon by firing arrows at her. Blizzardis aimed an arrow at the dragon's left eye and struck it perfectly. The dragon, screaming in pain, retreated from the Snowites to try and relieve her discomfort.

"Prince Zaaki, come quick," Blizzardis called, waving at Strongheart.

Strongheart flew the Prince to Blizzardis, while the rest of the Snowites went to hide. Blizzardis promptly described the dragon to the Prince, explaining it was the Leo Dragon, a dragon with the face and skin of a leopard. Her skin deflected nearly everything and if she touched someone, she could replicate their body and transform into their clone for as long as she wanted. This dragon was ruthless and would fight until she succeeded or was met with death. Blizzardis informed the Prince that the only way to kill this beast was to cut her head off with the Royal Sword of Luella.

"Thank you, Blizzardis you have helped me a great deal. Now do one more thing for me before the Leo Dragon returns. Go and hide with your men," Prince Zaaki insisted.

Prince Zaaki saw that Blizzardis did not want to leave his side, thus he firmly said, "That is an order."

Blizzardis reluctantly followed the Prince's instructions and hid with his men.

PRINCE ZAAKI AND THE ROYAL SWORD OF LUELLA

Star was hiding behind a glistening red sand hill with Honeypower. Star patted Honeypower on her back and began to stroke her luscious pink hair.

"I hope the Prince doesn't get hurt," Star said, worried for the Prince's life.

"He will be just fine. The Prince is—" Honeypower was interrupted when a black bag was thrown on top of her. Star hysterically tried to break open the bag and free Honeypower but was captured from behind. Star kicked her right leg backwards at her attacker and attempted to aim the machine gun that she was carrying across her shoulder at her faceless attacker. She screamed out to the Prince and Strongheart for help until the attacker knocked the gun out of Star's hands, seized Star, and covered her mouth with tape. Star tried desperately to thrash the attacker, but the attacker called for aid. Before three men wearing the official army uniform of Luella captured Star and put her in a black bag, she noticed the first attacker was a woman wearing a long, dark purple cloak. Four more men in army uniforms helped carry Honeypower and Star away from the beach and out of sight whilst the mysterious woman picked up the machine gun and took off her hood to reveal long, golden-brown hair. She then removed her cloak and buried it in the sand. She stood up, dusted all the sand off her clothes, which matched Star's clothes, and peered out to see where Prince Zaaki was.

"Men, take them to my father without delay. I will return with the Prince," the secretive woman called out to her men.

When her men had disappeared, she walked a few meters away from the sand hills and chose a patch of sand where she placed the machine gun continuing a few meters further. The woman, who was the spitting image of Star, ripped her dress to look as if she had been attacked and then removed a dagger hiding under her dress. She cut her left hand and let the blood flow, stowing away the dagger again. Realizing that the sand was covered with foot prints, she blew a ferocious turbulent wind from her mouth, turning in a circle, eradicating all the evidence of the kidnapping. She then lay down on the soft sand and feigned unconsciousness.

The Prince took his sword from his belt, raised it to face level, and held it tightly with both hands. He began to chant, "Give me the power to defeat the Leo Dragon."
The sword began to beam bright silver, twirling around the Prince, spinning him off the ground and turning him in complete revolutions a few times before disintegrating and leaving the Prince hovering a few inches above the ground.

The Prince whispered instructions to Strongheart whilst waiting for the Leo Dragon to reappear. Strongheart did as he was ordered, and hid behind a sand hill.
"Come out and show your face! I am waiting for you!" the Prince yelled to the Leo Dragon as he hovered above a patch of sand on the beach.

All of a sudden, the Prince saw the Leo Dragon hurtling

towards him so he ran in the air towards the dragon and, as he picked up speed, he rose higher above the ground and began to fly towards the dangerous creature. The Prince came face to face with the Leo Dragon and raised his sword, cutting the dragon's left wing. The dragon blasted a stream of fire but the Prince dodged to escape the yellow flames. As he ducked, he accidently swiped his hand across the stomach of the dragon. The Leo Dragon disappeared mid-air and a clone of the Prince appeared in its place. The Princes entered a sword fight, hovering in the air. Prince Zaaki scarred the face of the dragon disguised as the prince with his sword and forced him to do three back flips. The Leo Dragon touched the cut on his cloned face and saw blood on his finger, which made him furious. Enraged, he flew towards Prince Zaaki, roaring fire out of his mouth, and fiercely slashed his sword against the Prince's sword. Strongheart watched from a distance before rocketing to aid Prince Zaaki.

Strongheart, confused, could not decide who the real Prince was as both belted out, "It's me Strongheart, I am the real Prince!"

One of the Princes continued to say, "Come and stand by my side, Strongheart, and aid me in killing the imposter. He is the evil one."

Strongheart, knowing that the real Prince would not ask his help in fighting the dragon, stood by the real Prince, who had ordered him to stay hidden and protect Honeypower and Star.

"Go back to Star at once, Strongheart," Prince Zaaki exhaled as he swiped his sword against the disguised dragon's left shoulder, ripping his shirt.

"I cannot, Your Highness; I am here to protect you. Tell me what to do!" Strongheart demanded as he watched the two identical Princes battle it out in the sky.

"Fine, meet me on the ground and as we planned, do what I said," the Prince said as he watched Strongheart descending to the ground. While distracted, the cloned Prince took the opportunity and slashed his sword across the real Prince's right leg, wounding him.

Prince Zaaki instantaneously plummeted to the ground, holding his injured leg. Blood poured from the cut, so he ripped the sleeve off his shirt and tied it around his leg to cease the bleeding. The cloned Prince followed him and landed, but Strongheart came from behind and kicked him across the back of his head. The cloned Prince's legs gave way and he fell, unconscious, to the floor.

"Well done, Strongheart. Hold him down so when he wakes I can question him," the Prince dictated.

Blizzardis and his men came out of hiding and marched towards the Prince. The fake Prince, still unconscious, vanished for a mini-second before reappearing as the evil Leo Dragon once again. Slowly waking from her concussion, the Leo Dragon tried to roar as she got up but failed miserably.

"Who sent you? How did you know to locate me here?" the Prince demanded, digging his sword into a small yellow spot on the dragon's neck.

PRINCE ZAAKI AND THE ROYAL SWORD OF LUELLA

The Leo Dragon did not answer but instead tried to stand on her webbed feet. The Prince, not allowing the Leo Dragon to stand, pinned her down with his sword pressing deeper into her neck.

"Answer me, answer me now!" Prince Zaaki insisted. Strongheart added, "You had better answer the Prince or he will cut you up into a thousand pieces and scatter your remains all over the sea so that no one will ever find you."

The Leo Dragon looked at the Prince and laughed before closing in on the Prince's ear and whispering, "I will never tell you who my master is, but I will tell you that she will win this battle and rule this Kingdom."

The Prince's anger was amplified and he sliced the dragon's gigantic head off in one powerful attempt. The Leo Dragon's body disintegrated into a hot, sticky, substance that turned into yellow flames and burnt for a few minutes before evaporating into a puff of smoke and disappeared in the air. The head of the Leo Dragon leaked yellow blood from the neck. Blizzardis took a little box out from his pocket, lit a match, and threw it inside the dragon's head. Within seconds the head exploded into a ball of yellow fire and vanished.

"Okay now I must go and find the Sizzlites," the Prince told Blizzardis and Strongheart. "Time is not on our side but I want us to invade the General and his men posthaste and end this wickedness."

"Let me go and get Honeypower and Star," Strongheart said as he flew over to the sand hills.

"Okay, I am going to find out the exact location of the Sizzlites. VS, please show where the Sizzlites reside," the Prince ordered his VS watch, bringing his hand up to his face to see the screen.

"Your Highness, here is the location of Sizzi Village. You must follow this path and it will lead you to the Sizzlites." The VS described the directions and highlighted the path on the video screen.

"Good. Thank you VS. That will be all for now."

The Prince summoned Blizzardis and informed him that as soon as Strongheart returned with Honeypower and Star he would go to the Sizzlites. Prince Zaaki commanded Blizzardis to stay on the beach with his men and take good care of Star until his return.

chapter Thirteen
XIII

"They are not here!" Strongheart bellowed as he flew back to the Prince. "Star is gone! Honeypower is gone!"

"What do you mean, they are gone? Strongheart, go and search again. I will join you in my Zoktransporter," the Prince ordered as he ran towards his vehicle. "Blizzardis, take your men and search for them on land!"

Blizzardis divided his men and told each group to go in different directions and search for Star and Honeypower while Prince Zaaki flew the Zoktransporter up into the sky to scan the beach. Strongheart flew alongside the Prince, blaming himself for not staying with Honeypower and Star. In the corner of his eye Strongheart saw something lying motionless on the sand and flew down to check it out. Prince Zaaki followed Strongheart to investigate.

Strongheart landed and galloped to the side of the unconscious woman. The Prince landed the Zoktransporter and asked Strongheart if it was Star.

"Yes, it's Star! Star, wake up!" Strongheart nudged her slightly with his hoof but the woman, identical to Star, did not respond.

The Prince finally reached the Star look-a-like, knelt down by her side and calmly spoke to her as he held her left hand. "Star, please wake up. Strongheart, can you see anything around here to give us an idea on what happened?"

The woman disguised as Star rubbed her eyes as she came to. The Prince, relieved to see she was alright, asked her if she knew where Honeypower was. Star shook her head.

"I was hit across the back of my head and I must have been knocked out. That's all I remember. I'm sorry. I don't know where Honeypower went," she said as the Prince helped her stand up.

"Did you see anything unusual before you were hit?" Strongheart asked impatiently.

"No, I was just crouching down next to Honeypower, watching you fight, when it happened," the imposter lied.

"Prince, I need to keep looking for Honeypower," Strongheart said, unsatisfied with the woman's response. He flew away angrily to search the beach.
Prince Zaaki called out to Strongheart, "I will accompany

you, Strongheart! Wait for me."

The Star impersonator, not wanting Prince Zaaki to go with Strongheart, made her legs wobble and feigned falling into the Prince's arms. The Prince, concerned, forgot Strongheart's search for Honeypower.
"I think you'd better sit down in the Zoktransporter and rest," Prince Zaaki said softly as he led her to the vehicle and sat her down in the passenger seat.

"Prince Zaaki, please stay with me, I don't want to be alone. I am worried that whoever took Honeypower and tried to take me will do it again."

"How do you know they took Honeypower, Star?" Prince Zaaki queried.

"Eh well, Honeypower would have shown up if she wasn't kidnapped," she answered hesitantly.

Prince Zaaki knelt on the sand and gazed into the eyes of the woman sitting before him. He just wanted to feel the care and warmth that he had felt the night on the floating balcony. He didn't feel Star's sincerity and was puzzled.

"What's wrong?" the woman asked, noticing a look of confusion on the Prince's face.

"Nothing," the Prince quickly replied. "No, it's nothing. Are you feeling better now? Will you be alright if I go and help Strongheart locate Honeypower?"

"I am much better now," she replied. "But can I stay with

you? I want to go with you to search for Honeypower."

With that response, the Prince agreed, leapt into the driver's seat of the Zoktransporter, and within a flash started the engine and flew into the sky in search of Honeypower. As the Prince looked out his window down at the vast beaches of Luella, he noticed a path that looked as if it went under the Souls Sea. Curious, the Prince angled the Zoktransporter down slightly to explore further. The path was made from red sand and did not end when it reached the Souls Sea, instead leading straight into the sea under a tunnel of water. Prince Zaaki, curious to see this more closely, returned to his men.

The sun was about to set and the colours in the sky faded as it slowly descended into the waters of the Souls Sea. Strongheart, disconcerted, located the Prince landing the Zoktransporter near Blizzardis. He arrived by Prince Zaaki's side to tell him that he had searched the beaches of Luella and found no trace of Honeypower. The woman imitating Star sat silently whilst Prince Zaaki tried to reassure Strongheart that Honeypower was well and that they would find her. After Prince Zaaki comforted Strongheart for a brief period, he remembered that the path he found earlier would lead him straight to the Sizzlites. Deciding that he wanted to approach the Sizzlites alone, he left his passenger under the careful watch of Blizzardis. Without a moment to lose, Strongheart soared into the spectacularly red and orange sky with Prince Zaaki on his back, impatient to find his soul mate.

Strongheart soon drew near to the path, lowering altitude to just two meters off the ground, and advanced towards the Sizzi Village. The breathtaking path carved a ten-foot-high space through the Souls Sea, miraculously untouched by the water on either side. Prince Zaaki knew that magic had to be involved for this passageway to exist.

Suddenly, Strongheart halted at the magnificent amethyst gates that protected the Sizzi Village from unwanted intruders. Prince Zaaki leapt off Strongheart and walked towards a human-sized plasma screen on the right side of the gates. The plasma screen, sensing something was close, switched on. A female Sizzlite appeared on the screen, sitting in front of a wall-sized computer screen in a glass room behind the gates.

"How may I help you?" the Sizzlite asked in a computerized voice.

The Prince looked directly into the plasma screen. "We are here to see Goldy."

"Do you have an appointment?" the computerized voice continued.

"No but I need to see her now, it is extremely important!" the Prince cried, becoming frustrated with the questions.

"What is the nature of your business?" the Sizzlite interrogated, ignoring his pleas.

"It is urgent, please, I need to see Goldy. Tell her I am the Prince of the Kingdom of Luella, Prince Zaaki, son of the King!" The Prince stood tall and pulled his shoulders back.

PRINCE ZAAKI AND THE ROYAL SWORD OF LUELLA

The Sizzlite stopped questioning the Prince, put him on hold and contacted Goldy by blowing into her golden horn. A sweet piece of music hailed Goldy almost immediately to the glass room.

"Who is it?" Goldy asked the Sizzlite.
"It is Prince Zaaki and his horse, ma'am," The Sizzlite answered.

Goldy swam to the computer screen and introduced herself. "I am Goldy. How can I be of service, Prince Zaaki?"

"The Palace is in danger and I need your help," the Prince said. "My parents have been captured by General Scarytis and I am building an army to fight the General's army. Can you help?"

"Stand back, the gates are opening now," Goldy instructed the Prince and Strongheart as she pressed a small, red, diamond-shaped button on the side of the computer screen.

The gates opened and Prince Zaaki rode Strongheart through the entrance and to the glass room. He knocked on the glass door of the room, Goldy opened and admitted them inside.

"I know your parents very well. They are good decent people and if my people and I can, we will be honoured to help. Now, both of you put these in your mouths so that you can come with me to Sizzi Village and gather my women and men for battle!" As she spoke, Goldy handed the Prince two long, slim, glittering silver tubes bent at the end to form a piece that fit perfectly into their mouths.

The Prince placed the larger tube into Strongheart's mouth, and then put the smaller one in his own mouth, after which Goldy initiated the room to be filled with water, leaving them all submerged in the glass room. When the room was completely full of water, the ceiling opened up and they swam, following Goldy deep into the Souls Sea. The Sizzlite controlling the gates stayed behind and, when they departed, closed the ceiling with the touch of a button, returning the glass room to its original form.

Goldy, anxious to help the Royal Family, swam and led the Prince and Strongheart deep underwater until they reached the seabed, where the Sizzi Village lay. They swam past a gathering of ivory-coloured balloonfish with round black eyes, and two electric blue sea turtles treading water at a leisurely pace. Coral covered a vast majority of the seabed, in all different shapes with a multitude of colours permeating through the water resembling an underwater rainforest. Prince Zaaki held onto Strongheart's left wing, letting his much faster companion pull him through the water.

To the Prince and Strongheart's surprise, they arrived at the top of a pink bubble housing an enormous village; Sizzi Village. As she swam down to the entrance, Goldy glanced to her right to see an exotic breed of fish that was fast approaching them. This group of a hundred tiny little purple circle fish, known as Wheelyfish, with a green dot in the middle of their body for an eye, startled Strongheart when they zoomed past him at a great speed. Goldy described this friendly circle fish to the Prince, as gentle creatures who alert the Sizzlites of any intruders in the Souls Sea. She led them into the bubble encompassing Sizzi Village and came to a halt.

"Here we are, Sizzi Village, the land of the Sizzlites,"

Goldy introduced the Prince and Strongheart to her home.

Goldy blew into a delicate, transparent horn and within a few seconds, all the Sizzlites left their coral homes, swam in uniform, and gathered around a tall rectangular coral in the centre of Sizzi Village. The coral was changing colour from green to dark green, slowly turning to black. Goldy instructed Strongheart and Prince Zaaki to follow her onto the rectangular coral, used as a platform, to address her villagers.

"Quiet, quiet, please! Danger is lurking as you can all see; the coral is changing to black. This is Prince Zaaki, the son of King Zok, and his flying horse, Strongheart. They have come to us today in need of our help. I am going to pass you onto Prince Zaaki now who will explain to us all what has happened to the Royal Family," Goldy presented Prince Zaaki to the Sizzlites urgently.

"General Scarytis has overtaken the Palace with the help of Luella's army," The Prince announced. "My father and mother, the King and Queen of Luella, have been captured and are being held in the basement of the Palace. So far, I have been attacked by three different dragons sent by the General, I assume. I am building an army to fight the General and his army. The Snowites have joined and they are, as we speak, waiting for me on the beach. Now I come to you for your help.

I need an army. Who is prepared to fight for the King of Luella?"

Suddenly all the Sizzlites shouted out, "We will fight.

Long live the King! Long live the King! Long live the King!"

The Sizzlites all lifted their hands up high and continued to chant for a few more moments. Prince Zaaki, overwhelmed at how many people admired his father, glanced at Goldy. She gave him a reassuring nod in agreement with her people.

Goldy moved closer to the Prince and whispered, "We will now come up with you to land, which means that all the Sizzlites, including me, will need to go through the transformer. There are two thousand Sizzlites who will go up to join your army, so we will need a few hours to transform."

"What is that?" the Prince asked through his mouthpiece.

"It is a room that we must pass through that will allow us to emerge on land. It gives us temporary human form so that we may breathe on land and walk on land as you do," Goldy answered.

Although the Prince had read about the Sizzlites and knew that they were magical humans who lived underwater, the wonders of the Kingdom of Luella never ceased to amaze him. Strongheart impatiently nudged Prince Zaaki so that they could return above ground. The Sizzlites made their way out of Sizzi Village and up towards the glass room where they all transformed into full humans with legs and all the body parts needed to function on land. Strongheart started to swim towards the entrance of the Sizzi Village with the Prince clutching onto his wing. Whilst Prince Zaaki was being pulled through the water, he noticed Goldy ordering five Sizzlites to remain behind and guard Sizzi Village. When the final few Sizzlites descended out of their village followed by Goldy, Strongheart, and Prince Zaaki, the five guards of Sizzi Village closed its gigantic pink doors.

"Go to the glass room and my guard there will let you out onto the land of Luella. Go now. We must go through another room and we will meet you on the beach that leads to the path that led you here," Goldy advised Prince Zaaki and Strongheart as she and the Sizzlites turned and went in the opposite direction.

Strongheart swam straight up towards the glass room, speeding through the water. Very quickly, they reached the glass room but were unable to capture the Sizzlite's attention. Unsure where the door was or where to knock, Strongheart swam around the glass room in search of an opening or a hidden lever.

"Look over there." Prince Zaaki pointed to a small bump in the glass wall.

Strongheart swam to it and the Prince pressed down on it until the ceiling of the glass room opened and they swam inside. The Sizzlite hastily shut the ceiling tight, and the water that came gushing in with Strongheart and Prince Zaaki disappeared off the floor of the glass room. Prince Zaaki, relieved that he could now remove the tube from his mouth, asked the Sizzlite to open the gates of the Souls Sea and allow them to depart and return to the beach. The Sizzlite obeyed and they exited along the path that led them to the Sizzlites.

Chapter Fourteen
XIV

Nightfall crept its weary eyes upon the Kingdom of Luella as Prince Zaaki and Strongheart returned to the area where Blizzardis and his men had set up camp for the night. The Prince, after finding Star comfortably asleep in the Zoktransporter, walked over to Blizzardis and sat down on the red sand by his side, totally worn out. Blizzardis asked the Prince what happened in the Souls Sea. Prince Zaaki recounted his expedition while they waited for the Sizzlites to join them.

Strongheart, worried about Honeypower, stood silently behind Prince Zaaki and gazed up into the sky, wondering and wishing for her to appear and fly towards him. Mourning his lost soul mate, he fell asleep dreaming of her.

Prince Zaaki looked behind him to find his companion

sleeping and, out of the corner of his eye, saw movement nearing where they sat. The Prince could not make out what it was and stood to walk closer.

"I can't believe it!" the Prince exclaimed, astonished at what was drawing near.

"What, what is it? Is it the Sizzlites?" Blizzardis asked, unable to see in the darkness of the night.

"Yes, it is Goldy and her Sizzlites. Look at that, they have legs," the Prince laughed and then carried on to say enthusiastically, "Good, now we have one thousand and two hundred Snowites, and two thousand Sizzlites. All we need now is the Magnetians to join my army so that we can finally proceed home and reclaim the Royal Palace."

The Star impersonator awoke and quietly crept to listen in on the Prince's conversation to see what the Prince and Blizzardis were watching and waiting for. In the distance, she witnessed an army marching towards them and realized that Prince Zaaki was creating a colossal army from the villages of the Kingdom of Luella. She then looked at the Snowites, most asleep and a few guarding the camp, and at the Sizzlites closing in. Without hesitation, the false Star obtained her VS from her pocket and turned it on.

"Prince Zaaki is constructing an army and he will be moving north towards the Palace tomorrow. He has the Snowites and the Sizzlites but there are no Magnetians yet. They have set up camp for the night on the beach near the most north-eastern branch of the River Tara. Send me my two Sehhra Dragons to meet me in Magnetia tomorrow. We shall stop them before they reach the Palace and I shall reclaim what is rightfully mine, the Royal Sword of Luella!" The false Star sniggered at the end of her speech and placed her VS back in her pocket, checking that the Prince and Blizzardis hadn't heard her.

This fallacious woman, wrongly mistaken for Star by His Royal Highness and his men, decided to capture the Prince's attention and cried out. Impulsively, the Prince turned back and ran towards the Zoktransporter. Just before he reached the Zoktransporter, he detected Star crouched down on the sand and, without a second thought, hoisted her up and carried her to the camp wordlessly. The thought that this was not Star ruminated in the Prince's mind as he carried her. She seemed much heavier all of a sudden. To reassure himself that he was just imagining, he gazed into her eyes, desperately trying to find the connection they had once shared. Prince Zaaki knew that, when he looked into Star's eyes, he could glimpse her good heart. The Star look-a-like sensed that the Prince was not easily fooled and suspected that she was not the love of his life, so she quickly closed her eyes and faked falling unconscious.

"Star," Prince Zaaki whispered, laying her down on the sand alongside the weak campfire.

Prince Zaaki fetched a soft, green, woolen blanket from the back of his vehicle and covered the sleeping woman before him. He watched her for a few more moments before returning to Blizzardis, shrugging off the accusation he had conjured in his mind and reassuring himself that the woman he had just comforted was, indeed, Star, affected by the recent attacks on her and the Palace.

"Is she alright?" Blizzardis asked.

"She will be fine. She is still shell-shocked from earlier," Prince Zaaki said with a puzzled look on his face.

"Your Royal Highness, Prince Zaaki, the Sizzlites at your service," a voice proclaimed, before Blizzardis and the Prince turned to see Goldy in human form.

Goldy was more alluring in human form, with her army of Sizzlites following her, now a golden colour with effulgent pink eyes. She was riding on the back of her enticing water leopard, Talgy, who had the most beautiful white fur coat covered in large, golden spots, and dazzling, unclouded, sky-blue eyes. Talgy was an exceptionally fast athlete and could leap or swim across small rivers and huge ravines. The Sizzlites' captivating pulchritude reflected the beauty of the enchanting Souls Sea. Every silver Sizzlite with golden hair exuded elegance and exquisiteness as some marched and the rest rode their black and white water leopards behind Talgy, carrying their leader. Goldy had two muscular female Sizzlite guards, Galla and Coura, also riding by her sides.

"Goldy, please send your army towards the camp where the Snowites are resting. I want to see you and Blizzardis privately," the Prince dictated.

Goldy instructed Galla and Coura to take the Sizzlites to where the Snowites temporarily resided. Prince Zaaki silently watched the Sizzlites and the Snowites merge. "Goldy, Blizzardis," the Prince said, looking at them both and then continuing. "I believe that we may have an intruder among us. I am not certain, but I have a feeling that Star may not be whom I thought. Ever since Honeypower disappeared, Star has looked different. I cannot make it out and I am not willing to take any risks for the Kingdom, hence I have decided that we send two men ahead to take this letter to Zaeem, the leader of the Magnetians. He will organise the Magnetian army to meet us a few miles south of the Palace tomorrow in the middle of the day. Blizzardis, do you have two men ready and rested for this journey?"

"I will send two of my quickest men immediately," Blizzardis concurred, and ran to fetch two of his men.

Goldy, confused, questioned the Prince, "Prince Zaaki, who is this Star person you talk of? Is she part of an army?"

"No, no, she is not part of any army," Prince Zaaki clarified. "She is my mother's lady-in-waiting. I met her back at the Palace. She was sent by my mother to deliver a letter to me. Since Honeypower's disappearance I have a strange feeling she is different in some way. She is not the Star I met back at the Palace. Forthwith I want you to keep a watchful eye on her."

"What happened to Honeypower?" Goldy asked.

Just as Prince Zaaki was about to answer her question, Blizzardis approached with two of his men, dressed and ready for their mission. Prince Zaaki handed them the letter he had written to Zaeem and carefully explained how to get to Magnetia and where to find Zaeem's home. After crucial preparation and instructions, the two Snowites departed for Magnetia, and Prince Zaaki and Blizzardis accompanied Goldy to the camp.

"I want us to leave in one hour. Get your men ready and packed. We have no time to waste if we are to meet the Magnetians tomorrow," Prince Zaaki said quietly.
"If that is what you wish, I will have my men ready," Blizzardis replied.

Blizzardis walked away from the Prince and ordered his men to prepare for evacuation of the beaches immediately to follow Prince Zaaki, their future King, into a battle of good against evil. The Prince looked at Goldy, patiently awaiting an answer to her question concerning Honeypower's disappearance.

"Goldy, we do not fully know what happened to Honeypower, except that she was kidnapped whilst we were under attack by the Leo Dragon as we arrived on the beaches of Luella," Prince Zaaki retorted.

Goldy inspected the Sizzlites and loudly ordered, "Sizzlites, please be prepared for departure in one hour."

Strongheart, a very light sleeper, was woken by the noise of the Snowites and Sizzlites preparing for departure, so he located Prince Zaaki and flew to his side. The Prince, relieved to have his companion at his side, patted Strongheart on the back and explained that they were leaving for the Palace within the hour.

"Is there anything I can do to help, Your Highness?" Strongheart asked solemnly, still saddened at the kidnapping of Honeypower.

"Yes, you could do me a great favour and wake Star up, as I have to ensure that my army is all equipped and ready to go." The Prince proceeded to say, "Let her wait for me in the Zoktransporter."

"I will wait with her and guard her until you return," Strongheart said boldly.

"Thank you Strongheart."

As Strongheart galloped away, the Prince, with determination in his voice, called out, "Strongheart, we will find Honeypower. I promise you!"

Strongheart nodded silently in agreement, advancing towards the Zoktransporter.

"Star, Prince Zaaki wants you to be ready for departure immediately. I will wait by your side." Strongheart moved closer to the Star replica.

"Where are we going now? Are we going to Magnetia? Is it just the Prince and I, or all of us?" she interrogated. Strongheart studied the woman attempting to pry information from him and sensed something was amiss.

"Well? Answer me, you fool!" the fake Star demanded furiously, stomping her right foot angrily on the sand. Strongheart quickly responded, "What's wrong Star? Why so impatient all of a sudden? That's not like you. The Prince is organising an army to defeat the General, so why don't you return to being your composed self or I will not allow you to ride with my Master in this vehicle. Do you understand me?"

Accepting that she had nearly blown her cover, the Star imposter concealed her anger and serenely apologized to Strongheart, sitting down in the passenger seat of the Zoktransporter. Strongheart listened to her apology and did not reply, but instead turned his back to the Zoktransporter and guarded the supposed Star until Prince Zaaki arrived.

Chapter Fifteen
XV

Prince Zaaki led his already substantial army along the River Tara, the Snowites gliding across the water, the Sizzlites riding on their water leopards, and Strongheart flying alongside the Zoktransporter. The red sun was awakening, beaming its dazzling rays on the Kingdom of Luella as morning threatened. The Prince was operating the Zoktransporter whilst Star anxiously awaited their arrival at Magnetia.

The silence was profoundly disturbing as Prince Zaaki kept his eyes focused on the window screen in front of him whilst navigating the Zoktransporter. The Star imitator sneaked a look at her VS to see if she had received a message to inform her that her plan was underway. Out of the corner of his eye, Prince Zaaki noticed her abruptly hide her VS in her pocket.

"What's that?" the Prince questioned.

"What? Nothing, eh where are we going?" Star hastily changed the subject.

The Prince even more convinced that something was not right with Star, decided that he did not want to let her know their destination. He did not answer. Quietness emerged once again in the Zoktransporter.

Star's glare at the silent Prince intensified as she tried not to let her anger overcome her. Prince Zaaki peered down at the astounding sight of Goldy and the Sizzlites riding their water leopards on the land by the side of the River Tara, where Blizzardis and the Snowites skied along the river's surface. As soon as the Prince returned to look at Star, he felt her anger piercing through her eyes, so he decided to swiftly manoeuvre the Zoktransporter in a three-hundred-and-sixty degree loop before descending to just above Blizzardis. The Prince pressed a button, which opened his triangular window, and leaned out.

"Blizzardis, a little further up we will bend away from the River Tara. Are your men alright?"

Blizzardis nodded in acknowledgement and continued forward along the River Tara with the Snowites.

Suddenly Prince Zaaki made a fast, steep dip down towards Goldy, not allowing the imposter sitting by his side to take a breath. The Prince advised Goldy with the same instructions he had given Blizzardis, and then piloted the Zoktransporter to a higher altitude. The Star replica sighed deeply and removed her hands from the tight grip she had on the side of the vehicle.

"Oh my, that was…" The Star impersonator paused for a moment to think of the right word, and then finished with, "entertaining."

"Star, do you remember that night we had in the Palace before I departed on my journey?" Prince Zaaki probed, curious to hear her response.

"Of course I remember it, how could I forget, Prince Zaaki? I had so much fun dancing with you all alone on the floating balcony," she replied.

The Prince gazed into his supposed love's eyes and spoke softly. "Oh Star, I am so glad it's you. I thought… well, I thought that you might not… or that you were… anyway, it's not important."

"Yes I am definitely Star. It's me. Who did you think I was?" the Star replica queried.

"The important thing is that you are safe. And I told you not to call me Prince Zaaki," he graciously reminded her, after hesitating for a moment.

The Star replica quietly nodded, thinking of what he might have asked the real Star to call him. She wondered if there was a nickname he wanted her to call him. While she was still thinking, Prince Zaaki let go of the steering wheel and placed his arms around her in a tight embrace. As he hugged her, he noticed a tattoo on the back of her neck towards her right shoulder that resembled some kind of animal.

The Prince reminisced the night he had danced with Star, trying to recall a tattoo on her shoulder, but was interrupted when the woman in his arms gave him a light push to draw his attention to the Zoktransporter as it began to descend sharply. Without hesitation, Prince Zaaki grabbed hold of the steering wheel and pulled the Zoktransporter horizontal. Strongheart suddenly appeared in the Prince's window to alert him to the turning ahead. The Prince glanced down at Blizzardis and Goldy to ensure they were also preparing to leave the River Tara. Blizzardis and his men began to jump onto land and exchange their water ski boots for normal hiking boots. Goldy halted the Sizzlites and requested that each Snowite accompany a Sizzlite on their water leopard. Blizzardis joined Goldy on her magnificent creature.

"Why are we not travelling along the River Tare anymore? What are you doing?" the Star impersonator asked.

"We are headed for the Palace. Calm down, don't fear the General and his army, I will protect you," Prince Zaaki reassured her.

The Prince looked at her startled, horrified face and continued to say, "We will defeat the General's army and rescue my parents."

The fake Star nodded in silence as her plan was disrupted. She hastily conjured another plan to stop the Prince from reaching the Palace with his army. She needed him to land the vehicle at once. She immediately covered her mouth with both hands, leading Prince Zaaki to believe that she was about to vomit. Prince Zaaki looked down at the Up-Pine Forest and landed the Zoktransporter with a thump, opening the doors swiftly to allow his passenger to disembark. Wasting no time at all, the Star impersonator ran to a cluster of towering purple trees.

"Will you be alright? Do you need me to assist you with anything?" Prince Zaaki asked reluctantly.

"No, no, I will be quite alright by myself. Stay there!" the false Star ordered.

Blizzardis, riding with Goldy on her water leopard, arrived near the Zoktransporter and turned to stop their army behind them.

"Your Highness, is everything ok?" Goldy queried upon hearing someone grunting in the trees.

"Yes, yes. Star is not feeling very well. She is just sorting herself out behind the trees over there. Please go and check on her, Goldy," Prince Zaaki said as he pointed Goldy in Star's direction.

Goldy leapt off her dazzling creature and began to walk towards the woman behind the trees.

"Prince Zaaki, is this where the Magnetians will be meeting us?" Blizzardis inquired curiously.

"They should be here very soon. Well done, Blizzardis!" the Prince proclaimed.

The Prince looked towards Star and Goldy and then turned to Blizzardis and begged him, "Blizzardis, Star mentioned that my mother and father were in the basement with Futuris. I want you to sneak past the General and his army to locate my parents and Futuris and take them to safety whilst my army and I attack. When we commence attack, you must find a way in quickly, undetected."

Blizzardis accepted his task graciously as Prince Zaaki continued.

"After the attack is finished, I will meet you and my parents over where a clearing exists amidst a few trees. Blizzardis, can you see where there are eight gigantic purple pine trees positioned in the shape of a star?"

"Yes, I can," Blizzardis agreed, staring directly at the star-shaped cluster of trees.

"Wait in the centre of those trees for me," the Prince requested.

Goldy reached the gathering of trees and, before alerting the false Star to her presence, heard the replica talking to someone.

The Star impersonator whispered into her VS, "The Prince and his army are headed straight for the Palace. We are in the Up-Pine Forest, a few miles south of the Palace. Be ready for attack within the hour. I will try and hinder the Prince as much as possible and send for my Sehhra Dragons to come here now!".

Goldy did not allow the fake Star to know she had overheard the conversation, and instead hurried back to the Prince and Blizzardis to inform them of what she had heard.
The Prince saw Goldy returning and worriedly asked,

"What's wrong? Where's Star?"

"Prince, I think your assumptions on Star were correct. I just overheard her talking to someone on her VS, informing them of our whereabouts and commanding them to prepare for an imminent attack on the Palace. There are two Sehhra Dragons headed our way right this minute. My grandfather warned me of the Sehhra Dragons and that they are the creation of an evil sorceress who tried to kill the Royal Family a long time ago. You will know they are near when the air goes very dry and the sky turns sinister and dark. The Sehhra Dragon that my grandfather told me about was invincible and it was scared away by your late grandfather, King Zudus the Great," Goldy spurted out without pause. Nearly forgetting a few more facts about the Sehhra Dragon, she mentioned them under her breath.

"The Sehhra Dragon has fatally bright red eyes. She shoots beams of light from her eyes and mouth, and if theses beams of red light touch you, you are dead!"

Prince Zaaki, unnerved at what he heard, looked at Blizzardis then back at Goldy, contemplating a new plan of attack. After a long pause of silence, Blizzardis walked over to the Prince's army and ordered them all to prepare for an impending attack from the sky.

"She was using me all along. And I fell for her. She deceived my mother, my father, and me. I will not let her get away with this. Goldy, you and Blizzardis get my army ready for immediate attack. We have no time to waste as now we have lost the element of surprise," the Prince said before being interrupted by a familiar voice calling out to him.

"Your Highness, Protectius at your service," Protectius acclaimed, continuing to say, "I rode ahead of the Magnetian army to notify you that we are ready to fight for you and the Royal Family. Zaeem and Guardius will arrive very soon with our army."

Prince Zaaki grabbed hold of Protectius as they shook arms firmly.

"I am so glad you are here, Protectius. Come with me and I will introduce you to the Snowites and Sizzlites," Prince Zaaki stated with the hint of a grin.

A loud herd of horses carrying the Magnetians intruded the Up-Pine Forest and suddenly was brought to a standstill by Zaeem raising a sparkling silver sword and silver shield in his right hand .

"Zaeem, it is great to see you. Unfortunately, we don't have much time, so Blizzardis will get you up to speed with everything. He is the head of the Snowites. You, Guardius and Protectius come with me to meet Blizzardis and Goldy."

"Guardius, tell our men to stay here and rest for a few minutes, then follow us. Prince Zaaki, I didn't think we would meet again so soon. We are prepared to fight to the death for you, as you have proved your loyalty to our people," Zaeem valiantly declared.

Prince Zaaki rapidly introduced Zaeem and his men to Blizzardis and Goldy. Without delay, the leaders of the three villages sat down to discuss their plan of attack on the General and Star and her unknown associates.

"General Scarytis is mine. I want to fight him after his betrayal to me and my family. I will deal with him as I see fit," the Prince insisted as the leaders of the various villages of the Kingdom of Luella discussed strategy for combat.

The Prince beckoned to Goldy. "Goldy, please go and fetch Star. Tell her that we leave immediately. Also inform her that she will be riding with you, as Blizzardis will be accompanying me in the Zoktransporter. Do not let her know that we know she is against the Royal Family. Please hurry!"

Time was not on the Prince's side, so Goldy rushed to tend to the false Star and bring her to join the Prince and his army. Prince Zaaki waited until Goldy disappeared behind the trees and conversed with Blizzardis, Zaeem, Protectius, and Guardius to formulate a plan of attack on the General and his army and how to lure the two Sehhra Dragons to the Palace to slay them. Prince Zaaki knew that with the Royal Sword of Luella he could defeat these Sehhra Dragons successfully while Zaeem and Goldy, along with the Prince's new army, kept the General and his army occupied.

"Blizzardis you know what must be done," the Prince verified as he glanced at Blizzardis, and then said, "Zaeem, you get Goldy up to date with this plan on her return. Everyone understands where to go and what to do?"
They all nodded in agreement and hurried to order their army into position.

PRINCE ZAAKI AND THE ROYAL SWORD OF LUELLA

The Prince saw Goldy accompanying Star to her water leopard and gave her a nod as she walked past him.

"Goldy, I need you for a minute," Zaeem called out as soon as he detected her approach.

"Okay, Star, this is my companion. Jump on and I will be back shortly," Goldy said as she helped Star mount her water leopard.

Star gazed around and found the army that accompanied her from the beach to the Up-Pine Forest had quadrupled in size. Stunned at this mammoth army, she was left speechless, wondering where on earth they had come from. Goldy walked a few meters towards Zaeem and whispered instructions into her ear as they both kept a watchful eye on anyone attempting to listen in. Finally, everyone was poised and ready to attack. The Prince gave the keys of the Zoktransporter to Blizzardis and then rode forth on Strongheart, leading his army to confront the General, set his parents free, and acquire the Palace.

Prince Zaaki accumulated his colossal army on a clear stretch of land surrounded by the Up-Pine Forest. It was a splendid sight from high above, with the Sizzlites riding their water leopards, some carrying Snowite soldiers, and the Magnetians riding their horses gallantly. This assembly of men and women filled up the otherwise empty terrain and it looked as if they were part of the Forest, intertwined with its enormously tall, purple pine trees.

Strongheart flew Prince Zaaki up to about six meters

above ground so he could view the multitude of his soldiers and make sure all were ready to go forth in battle.

Prince Zaaki raised his sword and shouted to everyone, "Are you ready to reclaim the Kingdom of Luella?"

They all hollered, "Yes, we are ready!"

"Are you ready to attack and save the King and Queen of Luella?" the Prince asked loudly.

Once more they all replied, yelling, "We are ready! Long live the King and Queen of our great Kingdom! Long live the King and Queen of Luella."

"Then let us GO!" Prince Zaaki screamed and pointed his sword in the direction of the Royal Palace of Luella.

Chapter Sixteen
XVI

The Prince held his sword tightly as Strongheart flew him swiftly through the tense air. The sky suddenly became very dismal and electric red lightning cut the sky in half, right before their eyes. In a flash, the air dried up and Prince Zaaki felt parched, and soon after the Prince's army felt their mouths waterless. An unbearably deafening, high-pitched crackling infiltrated the Up-Pine Forest and the trees quivered in fear. But this noise did not jolt the Prince and his army, instead pushed them to go faster. Strongheart gawked behind at the gloomy sky and witnessed two red dragons with human witches' faces in the far distance.

The Prince wanted to lure them to the Palace, so Strongheart flew as fast as he could, whilst the Prince's army on land moved forward speedily, keeping up with the Prince, Strongheart, and Blizzardis in the Zoktransporter. Zaeem and Goldy were aware that they had company and needed to hurry their army to the Palace, and so encouraged them to pick up the pace. Goldy's water leopard leapt at such high-speed, in the blink of an eye she covered a few hundred yards of terrain. Star sat behind Goldy on her water leopard and the second she knew her two creatures were nearing she sneaked a malevolent laugh, which Goldy heard and felt, but remained unaltered.

The Prince became even more infuriated by the sight of the Palace straight ahead as he spotted the flag of Luella was no longer flying, but in its place a flag entirely black with the malicious Shadow Dragon and the atrocious red Sehhra Dragon on it. The Prince knew that at this precise moment in time he had to defeat the General and whoever else tried to prevent his family from reign in the Kingdom of Luella. But he also knew the importance of locating the magic pearls of Luella and guarding them from any and all thieves, so that villages and precious land would not be destroyed in search of the pearls by dragons, witches, and evil beings.

"Prince Zaaki, I am going to disappear behind the Palace now," Blizzardis quietly said, leaning out of the window of the Zoktransporter. "I will meet you when this is all over by the star."

"Yes, please be careful and stay undetected. Now go before we proceed for attack," the Prince responded under his breath.

Blizzardis flew the Zoktransporter around the left side of the Palace and vanished. The sky was turning darker and electric red lightning continued to strike like heavy rain drops. Strongheart had to manoeuvre to avoid being struck by the lightning. The Prince's army had to move, jump and leap quickly to avoid being hit by the never-seen-before deadly bolts of lightning.

The Prince halted his army and silently dispersed them into groups surrounding the whole Palace. He instructed all of them to wait whilst Strongheart flew the Prince over the Palace to see where the General and his army resided and where soldiers were standing guarding the Palace. The piercing, screeching sound was becoming louder as the Sehhra Dragons drew nearer. The Prince, knowing full well that this would alert the General, waited patiently for a few minutes during which Strongheart, carrying the Prince, circled the Palace to see from which entrance General Scarytis and his army would exit.

Abruptly General Scarytis exited the Palace from the second door on the right side into the gardens of the Palace, followed by a group of ten soldiers. A further hundred soldiers exited from the first door on the right side. All of a sudden the Prince noticed nearly a thousand soldiers exiting from all eight dome exits located at the front of the Palace into the front courtyard, armed and ready to defend. As all of this was going on, Strongheart alerted the Prince to the remaining soldiers scattered on the roof of the Palace.

The Prince murmured to Strongheart, "General Scarytis must still have more men inside the Palace waiting for us. Now fly to Zaeem and Goldy!"

Firstly, Strongheart flew down to where Zaeem was hiding with some of his men, awaiting the signal from

Prince Zaaki to charge in.

"Zaeem, you will break down the front gates of the Palace and enter from the courtyard. There are over a thousand soldiers awaiting you there. Tell your men to take no prisoners. Go on my signal."

Zaeem ushered a large group of the Prince's army to position. They all rode their horses and water leopards to the front gates of the Palace and came to a stop. All the while Strongheart flew the Prince to Goldy who was with the remainder of the Prince's army and positioned behind Zaeem and his group.

"Goldy you will take the rest of the army and attack from the gardens of the Palace over there," the Prince said as he showed Goldy the place he wanted them to strike.

"My water leopards can leap over that wall no problem. How many soldiers are inside?" Goldy asked.

"Close to a thousand, but I am sure there are probably more now. I will be with you because I have seen the General amongst the soldiers and he is all mine!" Prince Zaaki boldly stated whilst looking at Star, who was sitting like a ghost on Goldy's water leopard behind Goldy.

"What shall I do? Shall I go and seek your parents Prince Zaaki? I want to help!" The false Star tried to come across as helpful and sweet, but really she had a secret agenda that was to rid the Kingdom of Luella of all the Tars.

"No, you shall wait here. Jump off the water leopard and stay here. I will come and get you when I am finished. Find somewhere and stay unnoticed. Do you understand?" Prince Zaaki commanded aggressively.
The false Star was aided by Goldy off her water leopard and she walked away to hide behind some bushes to the west of the Palace. With no time to waste, Goldy instructed her soldiers where to attack and to prepare for the Prince's signal.

Strongheart and the Prince flew up into the doomed sky and the Prince raised his sword above his head with both hands, in his thoughts wishing for his sword to radiate a silver glow, which could be seen by all his army, to signal to his true soldiers of Luella to charge instantaneously. The Royal Sword of Luella beamed brightly and all around the Prince and Strongheart, the sheer luminosity that was created turned the sinister sky into a captivating vision for a few seconds. Zaeem and Goldy observed the signal and bellowed, "CHARGE NOW!"

The soldiers with Goldy were riding their water leopards and leapt over the great wall that divided the Palace gardens from the outside. With one gigantic leap, they entered the gardens of the Palace and commenced battle with the General's army, firing their machine guns and arrows. Without any dithering, the Prince's army, armed with swords, shields, daggers, bows and arrows, machine guns, and laser guns began to brutally slay the General's army. The General's army fiercely fought the Prince's army and wounded some of the soldiers. The Prince caught a glimpse of the General running towards a staircase that led to an open door to the kitchen of the Palace. Strongheart, without pause, flew the Prince to the staircase.

Prince Zaaki jumped off Strongheart and said, "I will fight General Scarytis alone. You go help Goldy and my army."

The Prince removed a golden arrow from the bag he was carrying on his back and raised the bow up in his left hand. He aimed at the General's leg and released the arrow, perfectly striking the General's right leg. The General paused to remove the arrow and continued forward, now with a limp.

Strongheart reluctantly allowed the Prince to run after the General alone and went to help Goldy and her army fight the General's army in the gardens.

Prince Zaaki ran up the stairs and into his home, keeping his eyes fixed on the General. General Scarytis ran round a corner in the grand hallway of the Palace and Prince Zaaki continued to follow him. Suddenly five evil army soldiers, wearing black suits from head to toe with only their evil red eyes piercing through the outfits, appeared and confronted the Prince. They began to kick and punch the Prince in fast motion and leapt into mid-air as they tried to kick the Prince. Prince Zaaki, doing somersaults and cartwheels airborne, skillfully with his sword cut their heads off one by one as they approached him. Prince Zaaki succeeded to fight off this party of wicked soldiers and persisted to locate the General. Prince Zaaki reached the magnificent staircase that led up to the royal suites. Gathering his thoughts for a moment, he decided to go to the basement as that was where his parents were being held and where the

General must have vanished to. Prince Zaaki went east of his marvelous staircase and entered the living area where he saw his mother's favourite green and purple rocking chair covered with pink petals in the middle of the room, swaying back and forth as if someone had run straight past it, nudging it. Prince Zaaki presumed himself on the correct path and exited the living area from a door straight ahead, arriving at a spiral staircase leading down to the basement. He carefully climbed down the stairs, bending down to see if any soldiers were lurking. When he reached the bottom of the spiral staircase, a soldier grabbed the Prince from behind and the Prince quickly kicked backwards and knocked the soldier unconscious. Prince Zaaki composed himself and made his way towards Futuris' quarters. He stopped in the hallway leading to Futuris and his parents and peered around the corner to see General Scarytis ordering three soldiers to kill anyone who tried to enter the basement. The three soldiers put their backs to the basement door and lifted their long metal arrows to their chests to vigilantly guard the hallway.

Out of the blue the General yelled, "Where are they? You imbeciles, they are gone!"

The General whacked the three soldiers over their heads with his hand and ran into Futuris' quarters again with his three soldiers closely behind him. The soldiers began to look in every corner of this large room, throwing Futuris' magic books on the floor and smashing his bottles of weird animal parts on the shelves. Prince Zaaki startled the General and the three soldiers as he ran in and launched into attack on the three soldiers, stabbing two of them through the heart and then cutting the third soldier's head off with one quick swipe of his sword. General Scarytis searched for a window or hidden door to escape through but failed, thus cornered and forced to fight Prince Zaaki.

"General Scarytis, how could you turn on my father after all he has done for you?" Prince Zaaki questioned the General as he placed the tip of his sword under the General's chin.

"Ha!" The general groaned and explained, "King Zok did not appreciate me. I protected and guarded the Royal Family since I joined the army as a young boy and what did I get in return? Tell me what did I get? It's time a new family took over the reign of the Kingdom of Luella. I will be King of the Kingdom of Luella and my daughter, the new Princess of Luella, will run the Kingdom. You have met her, I think."

"Who is she? Who is your daughter?" The Prince pondered for a minute and then angrily yelled out, "Star! Surely not Star?"

"Well done, Star is my daughter but her mother brought her up so she is not the one I speak of. Star unfortunately is an obedient servant of the late King and Queen of this land. I have another daughter! Sahara, Star's twin sister, will run the Kingdom." General Scarytis sneakily pulled out a sword from his belt. "Now I have told you this, I must kill you. Any last words before you meet death?"

Overwhelmed with information, Prince Zaaki shook his head and furiously dug his sword into the General's throat, saying, "I have no words to say to you except that you tell death hi from me."

The General raised his sword and struck the Prince's sword out of the way; quickly the Prince recovered and began a sword duel with General Scarytis. They fought for a short time in Futuris' quarters before departing and moving along the hallway, up the spiral staircase, along the grand hallway of the ground floor of the Palace and out of the grand entrance into the courtyard where Zaeem and a huge part of the Prince's army were fighting the few remaining soldiers of the General.
Zaeem glimpsed Prince Zaaki in a sword fight and shouted, "Prince, do you need assistance?"

"No, no, I am fine. Continue and then take your men to help Goldy in the gardens of the Palace," Prince Zaaki bellowed, out of breath as he kept his eyes glued on the General.

"Is that all you have?" the General egged Prince Zaaki. Finally, Prince Zaaki led the General to a circular wall in the middle of the courtyard that sloped upwards. In the centre of this circular wall was a water fountain. The Prince cunningly leapt onto the wall and, without any thought, back flipped over the General, landing behind him and stabbing his sword straight through his heart. The General fell forwards on his front and Prince Zaaki removed his sword.

Prince Zaaki gazed around to see that his army had defeated the General's soldiers, and without further ado rushed with Zaeem and their men to the gardens of Luella to find Goldy.

chapter Seventeen
XVII

"Zaeem, Goldy, please check the Palace and the grounds outside for any of the General's soldiers. Ensure none of Scarytis' soldiers are hiding anywhere in the Palace or surrounding it," the Prince initiated instructions and ran towards his companion. "I will be back soon."

Prince Zaaki leapt onto Strongheart's back and they flew hastily to the Up-Pine Forest. As they were flying over the forest, the Sehhra Dragons came into full view of Strongheart and Prince Zaaki. Forthwith, the Prince expeditiously raised his sword above his head. Prince Zaaki was eager to annihilate the Sehhra Dragons, so accordingly he summoned in Libnene, the old language of Luella, a spell that called for the Goddesses Ella and Lulu to give him the ultimate power to defeat and kill the two dreadfully wicked Sehhra Dragons.

Prince Zaaki:
"Uhtineh il owweh la ittol il beyouaff be darbeh!"

Promptly Goddess Lulu and Goddess Ella appeared, floating on two pure white clouds nearing Strongheart and the Prince. The lustrous, radiant golden beams that enveloped the Goddesses of the Kingdom of Luella lit up the otherwise caliginous sky. Simultaneously the two Goddesses put their hands in front of their faces, fingers directed towards Prince Zaaki, and began to send him the power of the sword through a bright golden beam exiting the tips of their fingers and entering the Prince's soul.

Goddess Lulu softly spoke to Prince Zaaki. "Zaaki, my dear Zaaki," she said. "You have the power to defeat the Sehhra Dragons. You have your great-grandfather, grandfather's and father's strength and courage to keep fighting until good wins. You will defeat evil and good will prevail!.."

Goddess Ella gave Prince Zaaki a loving and caring look before commenting on his power. "Zaaki, you are good and have a good heart. You have helped this Kingdom greatly already and have rid it of the evil General. You must believe in yourself and know that the power comes from within you. When you defeat the Sehhra Dragons and peace resides once more in the land of Luella, I will show you where the magic pearls of Luella are situated."

Prince Zaaki graciously bowed down to Goddess Lulu

and Goddess Ella as they floated away into the sky and disappeared. Strongheart interrupted the Prince with a neigh and alerted him to the Sehhra Dragons flying frantically towards him. Prince Zaaki mounted Strongheart once again and Strongheart flew him up to be level with the Sehhra Dragons. As they neared the Prince and Strongheart, the Sehhra Dragons commenced emitting flashes of deadly electric red lightning at Prince Zaaki and Strongheart, all the while Prince Zaaki and Strongheart both skillfully escaped being hit and fatally injured. The lightning was coming at them fast and dangerous, but they manoeuvred, Strongheart rotating and flipping three hundred and sixty degrees, as if someone had hit the fast forward button on them.

The false Star, who in fact was actually Sahara, Star's twin, was riding on one of the Sehhra Dragon's back and during the dragons' firing rage at the Prince and his companion, Sahara leapt off the dragon's back doing a double flip forward in the air before landing perfectly, standing vertically. Sahara vanished into the midst of the trees in search of the King of Luella, knowing that was the reason Prince Zaaki came to the Up-Pine Forest. Prince Zaaki was aware that Sahara ran into the Up-Pine Forest but could not stop her as he had two attackers trying fiercely to kill him. Prince Zaaki, quick-thinking as he was, whispered a plan into Strongheart's ear and without further ado made a huge pounce from Strongheart onto the back of one of the Sehhra Dragons. Consequently, Prince Zaaki jumped off her back and somersaulted over the Sehhra Dragon.

During his mammoth flip he stabbed the Sehhra Dragon in both her eyes thus blinding her. The injured Sehhra

PRINCE ZAAKI AND THE ROYAL SWORD OF LUELLA

Dragon screeched a high-pitched crackle and fell to the ground, crying for her sight. Not wasting a precious second, the astute Prince landed on the grassy terrain, ran so that he stood directly beneath the second Sehhra Dragon, and signaled to Strongheart. Strongheart understood his role and flew directly above the Sehhra Dragon posthaste. The Sehhra Dragon lost sight of Prince Zaaki. so instead aimed at Strongheart and shot ten flashes of lightning from her mouth every second at Strongheart who was positioned vertically above her. Strongheart flew like a speeding rocket out of the way and the lightning went up into the dark, gloomy sky.

"What goes up must eventually come " The Prince hesitated for a moment. "Down!"

And with these words the lightning that the Sehhra Dragon had fired out of her mouth came tumbling down on her. Prince Zaaki hurriedly moved away from both the dragons and took cover next to Strongheart behind a tree whilst the lightning killed both of the Sehhra Dragons and they evaporated into a sticky dark red goo on the ground. With their death, the sky returned to its original colour and the sun reappeared in the sky, lighting up the world with its strong bright rays.

"That's done, still one more though. Strongheart take me deeper into the Up-Pine Forest so that we find Sahara, Star's evil twin, and rid this Kingdom of evil once and for all!" Prince Zaaki climbed onto Strongheart.

Strongheart galloped anxiously in search of Sahara. "I can hear something, Your Highness. Can you hear it?"
"Yes, it's coming from over there! Quick go! Go!" The

Prince heard loud voices in the distance on his right; deeper into the Up-Pine Forest they rode, nearing the cluster of trees shaped like a star.

Strongheart heard a powerful horse neigh and recognized it which made him gallop crazily until he reached the trees positioned to form the perfect star. In the middle of this cluster of trees were Star and Sahara in battle. Honeypower was watching and trying to help Star but getting confused as to who was Star and who was Sahara. Prince Zaaki rode up to the two women in battle, jumped off Strongheart and stood between the women. Honeypower set eyes on Strongheart and galloped to his side and grinned overjoyed. Strongheart, ecstatic to see his love, neighed blissfully.

"Star? Which one of you is Star?" Prince Zaaki looked at the woman standing on his left. He gazed into her eyes and felt nothing. After which he turned and gazed into the other woman's eyes and immediately knew she was Star.

Prince Zaaki pushed Star towards Strongheart and told him to fly her away. "Take Star and Honeypower and go find my parents." Prince Zaaki's eyes flashed precariously. "Sahara, your failed attempt to fool me was pathetic. You really thought you could take my Kingdom from me?"

"Prince Zaaki, you and your precious title. You think everything in Luella is yours. My grandmother, Malicia, loved your grandfather but he didn't notice her. Instead he murdered her. She died trying to get back the pearls that belong to us. Now I will finish what my grandmother started," Sahara spoke wickedly.

"You are a sad, sad person if you are holding a grudge against the royal family because of your dead grandmother who, by the way, did not show love to my grandfather but in fact the complete opposite. She showed him hate and evilness. I cannot risk your threat to my Kingdom ever again, hence I must do what needs to be done and send you to join your grandmother. I will take no pleasure in this as you are Star's sister but you are both completely different. Star is kind and loving . I cannot believe you are of the same blood."

Sahara sneered at the Prince, triple somersaulted over his head and landed near a tree. Prince Zaaki instantaneously followed her, doing a quadruple somersault, and kicked her in the face as he landed. Not allowing Sahara to recover, Prince Zaaki made a right angle with his legs and kicked Sahara in her stomach, forcing her to fall to the ground. After a short moment, Sahara lifted herself up and back flipped over the Prince's head. Whilst she was airborne, Sahara kicked the Prince in the back of his head. She followed with repeated kicks to his back as he fell to the ground. Prince Zaaki was tired of fighting and wanted to see his parents so he stood up, swiftly rotated to face her and furiously kicked her in her stomach, which pushed her backwards. She landed on a branch that was perpendicular to the ground and it stabbed her through her chest. She died instantly and her body evaporated into a puff of grey smoke.

Prince Zaaki, relieved that he had finally defeated all evil in the Kingdom, called out for his mother and father. Strongheart and Honeypower reappeared carrying King Zok, Queen Tee-Tee, Futuris, and Star. Prince Zaaki, elated to see his parents alive and unharmed, ran towards them and hugged them tightly.

After which, Star ran to Prince Zaaki and he embraced her securely for a few minutes, glad that Star was alive and the connection they had was real.

"Zaaki, I am thrilled to see you. I prayed for your safe return. You have saved us all," Star said contently as she let go of him and he walked to his mother.

"Zaaki, I am so happy to see you. You saved us, and you saved the Kingdom of Luella. I am so proud of you. I love you, my darling, darling son!" Queen Tee-Tee said jubilantly as she hugged her son and kissed his cheeks over and over again.

King Zok was euphoric that his son rescued them and prevented the malevolent General and his malicious daughter from taking over the Kingdom. King Zok was speechless as he hugged his son tightly.

"Father, are you alright? Did they hurt you?" Prince Zaaki questioned his father, caringly.

"No, my son, we are all uninjured. You did well. You did very well. Now let us go home." King Zok placed his arm on Prince Zaaki's shoulder and walked with him as they all began their journey back to the Palace. Strongheart and Honeypower galloped slowly by their sides and Blizzardis flew the Zoktransporter at a leisurely pace, remaining near the King and Queen of Luella.

Chapter Eighteen
XVIII

The sun had set over the Palace gardens, leaving behind a glow of bright amber amongst the trees, plants and animals. Futuris had restored the magic of the Palace and it was once again enchanted, hence the royal waiters and royal guards hovering on their hover boards and the sparkling silver logs that hovered airborne in the grounds of the Palace before, returned allowing the striped electric blue and gold flamingo-legged zebras to enjoy hurdling the high logs as well as running across the shimmering, purple-grassed garden. This grand fortress, illuminated with tear-drop shaped lights that covered the entirety of the building, front and back, was filled with laughter and merriment as the Snowites danced and drank with the Sizzlites and the Magnetians. The grand Palace was breath-taking and alluring in the moonlight and meshed well with the extraordinarily large stars glittering the sky. The scent of contentment filled the grounds of the Palace and finally there was peace, at least for the near future.

King Zok and Queen Tee-Tee had invited the Snowites, the Magnetians and the Sizzlites for a huge celebration to offer their thanks and gratitude for their help and support. The Queen's animals stood on the sides of the grounds, watching and eating berries from the soaring pink trees that encircled the massive garden of the Royal Palace. Queen Tee-Tee organised the Royal Orchestra to play exciting music that suited the mood of the celebration perfectly.

The Queen had arranged the food, the entertainment, the seating and the decorations in the garden of the Palace. The Royal Orchestra was positioned in a semi-circle, surrounded by orange and silver roses, to the east of the garden, facing the guests. As the Orchestra played the arrangements organised by the Queen personally, the Catbirds began to hum along with the melody and produced a lovely calming ambience to the celebration whilst the roses released a scent of happiness and peace into the air.

Protectius was offered the post of new Army General by King Zok and had accepted it graciously, thus in charge of protecting the King, all the royals of the Kingdom, the Royal Palace, and most importantly the Kingdom of Luella. Protectius had already dispersed part of his massive army all over the Kingdom and some of his men were guarding every inch of the Palace which pleased the Prince immensely.

Prince Zaaki gathered Blizzardis, Goldy, Zaeem, Guardius, Protectius, Star, Strongheart, Honeypower, and his parents to make a toast. "I raise my glass to thank you all for your help in rescuing King Zok and Queen Tee-Tee and restoring peace and goodness back into our Kingdom."

"Hail the Tars! Long live the King of our great Kingdom!" They all cheered and drank their wine.

"Prince Zaaki, I have something that belongs to you. Come with me," Zaeem informed the Prince, placing his arm on his shoulder and guiding him away from the party to a quieter place in the corner of the great exotic garden where Bobby, Zaeem's little boy, stood shivering from fear.

"Your Highness, I am very sorry I took this from your bag. I, I, I..." Bobby, terrified, bowed his head.

"Well thank you for owning up, that takes a lot of courage. It was given to me on the condition that I return it hence I cannot give it to you. Bobby, from now on if you want something, you must ask first. Don't ever take without asking because that's wrong. Enough of that now, go and have fun! Go see the Queen's animals!" Prince Zaaki explained to Bobby.

Bobby gave Prince Zaaki a huge hug and looked up at him with his big brown eyes.

"Your Highness, can I just ask for one thing, if I may, your Highness?" Bobby asked in the sweetest manner.

"Of course, Bobby, what is it?"

"Can I have a go on your hover board? I have never been on one before!" Bobby exclaimed excitedly.

Prince Zaaki let go of his hover board and it magically turned horizontal and lingered in mid-air. Prince Zaaki stepped onto it and lifted Bobby off the ground and placed his feet safely on the hover board in front of him.

"I am going to take you on a ride above the Palace. Zaeem, we will see you shortly," Prince Zaaki yelled as he directed the hover board higher and higher into the clear night sky.

"Prince Zaaki I have a secret, I need to tell someone and you are someone who I hope can help," Bobby spoke fearfully.

"Please tell me you haven't stolen something else."

"No, its nothing like that," Bobby said.

"I will try to help, what is it?" Prince Zaaki asked curiously.

"It's about a secret friend I have. He transports himself with a blink of his eyes. His name is Fred, and he visits me regularly to see his father. His father is a Magnetian but he does not know that his son exists," Bobby explained.

"Who is his father? Do I know him?" Prince Zaaki quizzed.

"Yes, you do. It's Protectius, your Highness."

A speechless Prince Zaaki was momentarily taken aback with this news.

"I never knew Protectius was married."

"Yes, he was and still is. His wife ran away a long time ago, I think just before I was born. I always here father talking about Protectius and that he will never stop searching for her. When she ran away she was pregnant with Fred and she ran away because she has something wrong with her. She was worried that her child would also have this and so she ran away so that Protectius would not find out about this. Fred has this power as well and he is scared to show anyone, he made me promise to keep it a secret but I can't anymore. He needs help and so does his mother." Bobby, relieved to share this secret, let out a great big sigh.

"You must take me to Fred. He has a gift, Bobby, it is something to be cherished and nurtured. He should not hide and neither should his mother," Prince Zaaki expressed.

"He is here at the party. He followed us," Bobby confessed.

Prince Zaaki, not wanting to lose anymore valuable time, landed safely on the grass and began to search for Fred with Bobby. Bobby walked over to the buffet and looked under the tables and behind the trees, quietly calling out his name. Only a few minutes passed when Fred appeared, munching on some of the delicious food.

"What is it, Bobby?" Fred queried.

PRINCE ZAAKI AND THE ROYAL SWORD OF LUELLA

"I want you to meet Prince Zaaki. He can help you and your mother."

"How could you?" Fred asked as he vanished.

"Come back Fred. I am here to help you. You have a gift, please, I can help you and your mother." Prince Zaaki tried to beckon him back, "Don't be scared, your gift is special, you are special. Its not a bad thing, I promise, I will not harm you, I want to help."

Fred reappeared and nodded to Prince Zaaki. Prince Zaaki summoned the Goddesses with his mind and instantly they materialised in the sky. The Goddesses took Fred, Bobby, and Prince Zaaki to Fred's mother.

"It's over there, that's our home," Fred said, directing them.

Prince Zaaki knocked on the door of a rustic looking, small house in the middle of nowhere. A beautifully graceful lady opened the door slowly.

"Hello?" Jamilietta answered.

As soon as she caught sight of Fred, she hugged him tightly.

"I am Prince Zaaki and I am here because of your special gift. I want to introduce you to Goddess Ella and Goddess Lulu."

"What do you want? Please," a terrified Jamilietta begged, pulling Fred inside and starting to close the

door, she continued, "We don't have anything, just go."
"Please mother, listen to them. They want to help us," Prince Zaaki said.

"We have a special gift and it's not bad," Fred explained. "The Goddesses can help us. They told me there are others like us, we are not alone."

Jamilietta, trusting her son's intuition, reopened the door and let them in.

"Fred has been making regular visits to Magnetia to see his father and this tells me that you love him very much still. Protectius is a good man and will understand what you have and he will see it like we do, as something amazing. The Goddesses will take you to their school where you will learn to appreciate and understand your gift. I want you to trust me, Jamilietta," Prince Zaaki said, hoping she would agree.

Jamilietta gazed into her son's eyes, seeing that he was desperate for answers as to why he was different. Thus after discussing with the Goddesses what the purpose of the school was, Jamilietta decided it was best for her and Fred to go with them.

"We had better get back to the party. Your father will be wondering where we are." Prince Zaaki said to Bobby.

They landed in the Palace garden and Bobby thanked the Prince with a quick embrace before running off quickly to tell his sister and mother what happened.

"He's a good kid," Prince Zaaki said to Zaeem as they

watched Bobby dancing with his sister and mother.

"Yes, he is. Your highness, I think someone is looking for you," Zaeem said as he noticed Star searching the dance floor in the centre of the garden, giving the Prince a slight nudge towards her. "Go to her, I can tell she has your heart. Now be gone with you, I am going to dance with my wife! And remember to enjoy this spectacular evening!"

Unexpectedly a huge burst of fireworks invaded the peaceful night sky. Everyone halted to admire the incredible display of animal-shaped fireworks. Queen Tee-Tee happily gazed at all her pleased and stunned guests, feeling content that she accomplished a successful celebration for her people. The fireworks went on for the better part of an hour, leaving everyone speechless and astounded.

"That was truly spectacular! Now go!" Zaeem, still in awe of this magnificent night, encouraged Prince Zaaki to seize the moment.

"I'm going. I'm going!" Prince Zaaki said as he straightened his shirt and collar and made sure his hair was neatly pushed backed off his face.

Prince Zaaki handed his hover board to Zaeem and walked over to Star, staring at her elegant splendour as he extended his hand in front of her. Star was wearing a simple, yellow, backless dress that fitted her perfectly. Her exquisite golden locks of hair covered most of her naked back. Star gracefully accepted his hand and they began to dance. Without much ado, Prince Zaaki found himself holding Star in his arms swaying her gently from side to side, listening to a soft, slow song. Whilst the enormous glistening stars sparkled down on them, Prince Zaaki and Star filtered out all the noise surrounding them and were gladly lost in each other's intoxicatingly enticing eyes. Prince Zaaki gazed intensely into Star's eyes and saw deep into her soul, knowing that she was the one!

But as Star stared into Zaaki's eyes, she was confused between the love she felt for him and a hint of betrayal. In the back of her mind, she could not erase the fact that Prince Zaaki had killed her father and sister who were unbeknownst to her. She knew that he had no other choice but it still tormented her.

THE END

Heba Hamzeh

Heba Hamzeh is a mother of three extraordinary children and it was them that inspired her book. It all started one evening as Heba was reading a book to her son at bedtime. After finishing the book, her son asked for another story and in that moment Heba decided to create a story about a boy named Prince Zaaki. The following night her son asked for another Prince Zaaki adventure and so the Kingdom of Luella began to unravel. Forthwith Prince Zaaki bedtime stories became a ritual- a nightly occurrence - as her son would sit in bed with a huge smile on his face intently listening to Heba create a magical world full of mystical characters and mysterious places and battles. And so Prince Zaaki and the Royal Sword of Luella evolved and as you are reading this, Heba continues to create new characters and plots for her second, follow-on, book.

A note from the author: I hope you, the readers, enjoy this book as much as I did creating it and telling it to my son.